Dedication

To all of you who fell in love with the Carey family,
this book is for you.

Wonderful readers, thank you so much for reading along with the Carey brothers as they went about doing their crafty father's bidding… despite themselves, in some cases.

I hope you enjoyed your first few visits to Cowboy Point even half as much as I've enjoyed writing about it. I wish I could move there myself! I'm dying to spend some time at Mountain Mama Pizza and poke around the General Store, get coffee at Helena's cart, and wander the Farm & Craft Market on an endlessly blue and sunny summer day…

The good news is that there are more Cowboy Point stories coming your way, so there's no need to say goodbye. And while we'll be looking at the community and its delightful citizens through new eyes, I'm sure we'll see the Careys as we go. I love them too much not to check in on them from time to time.

Happy reading!

Prologue

"THERE'S SOME WEATHER coming in."

Zeke Carey looked up as his wife came into the room, speaking with a softness that was uncharacteristic for a woman so filled with enough thunder and lightning when she pleased that she was her own weather system. He smiled at her.

Because she was his favorite kind of weather and had been for a long, long time. So long now that he wasn't sure what he'd do if he found himself without his Belinda's many storms and seasons, sometimes all in one day.

He didn't intend to find out.

Zeke knew that she was talking about the Montana winter outside. It was a blustery night. There was an intense December wind rushing through the mountains that stood high above Paradise Valley, rattling the windows and bouncing off the sides of the house that was set down in the middle of the northern Gallatins. It was the sort of night that made a man want to settle in, maybe with a proper drink, and think a while on his life.

But he didn't need to cue up the good country music and get to thinking on his regrets, because Zeke was lucky enough to have precious few of those. And tonight the weather could do as it liked because he wasn't sure he'd ever felt more content, the wild Montana winter be damned.

He was stretched out on one of the beds that had once belonged to one of his five sons. They were all grown now and men in their own right, a sweetness that only grew as they lived their lives well, but tonight he had something almost sweeter. His two grandsons, three-year-old twins Eli and Levi. He'd been reading the boys a bedtime story and now they'd fallen asleep, curled up on either side of him like sweet little mirror images.

Looking a whole lot like their daddy, Ryder, and his identical twin brother Wilder had when they were that age.

"It smelled like snow earlier," he said in the same quiet way to Belinda, who'd come in to stand beside the bed now, beaming down at the scene before her.

Their sweet, funny, small boys were staying with their grandparents for Christmas this year, which Zeke and Belinda were over the moon about and didn't bother pretending otherwise. The twins' mother, Rosie, had another set of twins on the way—God bless her—and both she and Ryder were down the mountain in Marietta. They were staying in a rental not far from the hospital in the much bigger town on the valley floor because they expected her to give birth to her babies any day now and didn't want to try to navigate the treacherously slippery road down Copper Mountain in the darkest part of the year.

A win all around as far as Zeke was concerned.

"The snow should start coming down soon," Belinda told him, drifting closer so she could lean in and run a hand over one boy's cheek and the other's ruffled hair. "I've checked all the flashlights and set up the lanterns. And I saw you brought in more wood for the stove."

"We'll stay nice and toasty," Zeke assured her, though she knew that as well as he did. Because they always had before. Winter was no joke in these mountains, but it was no trouble, either, if a person was prepared.

He hadn't built this house, but he'd grown up in it. He knew it as well as he knew the stretch of his own skin across his back, the bones broken and mended inside his own body. They had a generator these days, because their boys had insisted upon it, but it would take a lot more than a Christmas snowstorm to get Zeke turning his back on the simple pleasures of an old-fashioned wood burning stove that could warm most of the house. Not to mention the pleasure of lantern light on a cold, dark night.

Simple joys that reminded him of a past long gone.

Thinking about that generator got him thinking about his sons. The three oldest he'd made with his sweet, lost-too-soon first wife, Alice. He'd promised her that he'd see to it that their boys would lead good, happy lives, and over the past year and a half he had made that happen. His oldest son and the wife he'd found by virtue of an old-timey ad in the paper had given birth to their first child in September. And now, even sleep deprived and filled with all the panic and devotion of the new parents they were, Harlan and Kendall seemed happier than most.

It made Zeke happy too.

His wild twins were doing well too. Wilder and Cat were enjoying their newlywed status, and Cat, who had always worked in her family's general store in town, had declared her intention to become a nurse and had started taking classes to bulk up on her prerequisites. Because not everyone went straight to babies, Zeke knew, and as long as they were happy, who was he to complain?

Yet.

Besides, he'd only realized in the last year that Rosie Stark's twin babies, the ones she'd had after college off in Texas and had moved home to raise, were Ryder's. He would have been happy to welcome the little boys into the Carey family no matter what happened between their parents, but he could admit that he'd hoped for what had ended up happening instead: Rosie and Ryder falling in love, marrying, and wasting no time expanding their little family.

And by extension, Zeke's family.

He had two sons with Belinda, too, though it was always funny to separate them out that way. Belinda had treated Alice's boys as her own from the day she'd met them, and while no one ever forgot Alice or ever would, Belinda had mothered them all. Boone, the oldest of the boys she'd given birth to herself, had gotten married to the woman he'd been in love with his whole life on Labor Day. He'd been resigned to call Sierra his best friend, and nothing else, while she soldiered on through an unhappy marriage—but the summer had changed all that. It was early days yet with them, Zeke knew. He couldn't get a read on whether they wanted to dive straight into making a family, or spend some more time basking in each other.

Either way, they were happy. And so Zeke was happy.

And, sure—had he engaged in the tiniest bit of deception to bring all this about? Damn right he had.

He had taken it upon himself to announce at Easter, the year before, that he only had a year to live. And yes, he'd already passed that year mark and was headed toward his second Easter of health and happiness despite his supposed diagnosis. Boone had already called him on the lie.

But Zeke couldn't come clean.

Because his youngest son, the charming and clever Knox, was still depressingly single.

He moved from the bed, shifting the little boys so that Belinda could cover them up with the cozy comforter and tuck them in, humming the same song she'd sung to all their boys over the years.

They stood there a moment, smiling down at the toddlers the way they had smiled down at so many of their children tucked up in their beds. And when they walked out of the room, they held hands as they made their way to their own bedroom.

Zeke didn't turn on the lights as they walked into the room, and not only because they were likely to go off soon. Together, he and Belinda went to the window, where he could see that the snow was already beating at the glass, swirling down in that relentless Montana fashion that made it clear it intended to keep going some while.

"Looks like it's going to be a minute before we get back into town," he said.

"I like being tucked up on the ranch at Christmas," Belinda murmured, gazing out into the dark. "Besides, all this snow means anything can happen."

Zeke pulled Belinda closer so he could wrap his arms around her and rest his chin on her head. Alice had been a sweetness that warmed from within. Belinda was a simmering fire that was never quite banked. She turned into him, running her hands down his back and nestling into him.

"We have to do something about Knox," Zeke said in a low voice.

"We're running out of time," she agreed. "Sooner or later one of the others is going to mention the fact that you've become an apparent miracle of medical science, and then what? How on earth will you convince that boy to settle down?"

Zeke laughed. "He thinks I'm dying and he hasn't been convinced yet."

"He's always been that way," Belinda said, but there was approval in her voice. "Hard-headed no matter how much he smiles his way through things. He gets that from my side."

"Right," Zeke drawled. "Because Careys are known for being pushovers. Not stubborn at all."

"It's a different kind of stubborn," Belinda maintained. "You know as well as I do that he wanted to leave Cowboy Point. Maybe even Montana. You might not have convinced him to marry and start on some babies with your little stunt, but he's still here. That's not nothing."

Zeke thought about his youngest. The most charming of the Carey brothers, some said. The most easygoing, others claimed, though that always made Zeke laugh. Because Knox was the only one of his sons who had been determined to go to college and had made it happen. Knox was the only one who had taken his high school football years, turned them into a scholarship, and had gone to the University of Montana on the other side of the Rockies in Missoula. He'd done well at UM as a college athlete and had also gotten excellent grades and a business degree.

Maybe he came off charming and easygoing to those who took him at face value, but Zeke knew better.

Knox was the only one of his children who could, if he liked, go anywhere to make his living. He was the only one who wasn't necessarily a rancher in his blood and bones, despite the land that had been in their family for generations. This wasn't to say that Knox didn't love the Carey family ranch or the years he'd spent working it side by side with his brothers—no matter that his brothers liked to pretend that wasn't the case.

Harlan was a salt of the earth kind of a man who had dedicated his life to High Mountain Ranch and would no doubt teach his children to do the same. Boone was made in the same mold, though he was more independent, and had opened his own artisan dairy that had already been a huge success. Wilder and Ryder were different. Wilder was happy to work the ranch and support his new wife as she chased her dreams, because he didn't have an ego the way some men did. Ryder, on the other hand, had made a name for himself on the rodeo circuit because he'd wanted something that was his, but he'd done that. Now he seemed perfectly content to build a family with Rosie and settle in.

The lives they'd lead were a lot like the life Zeke had led, and it was a damned good life.

But there were other ways to live this ranch life. Zeke knew that. Just like he knew that it was Knox who could change things up around here, if he stayed here. If he made a life here. It was Knox who had the big ideas about the kind of things they could do with the ranch so that his brothers didn't have to work themselves to death on this sometimes unforgiving land the way so many of their ancestors had.

The way he likely believed Zeke had, for that matter.

But he also knew that Belinda was right. Knox had a restlessness in him. His youngest needed a reason to stay right here in Cowboy Point, and that wasn't going to come from family pressure.

Or not only from family pressure.

What Knox needed was to get his head turned around, and Zeke was pretty sure there was only one woman around these parts who had ever managed that feat. He had to hand it to his boy—Knox had excellent taste and, like his father, clearly liked women that were much too good for him.

A secret to a happy marriage, and Zeke would know. He was on his second.

He'd spent a great deal of time trying to figure out how to hasten that head turning along, before his charming youngest son with his eyes on the horizon decided he needed to go somewhere else to make his way in this world.

Something that would break his mother's heart.

And Zeke's too, come to that.

But as the snow kept coming down, and the wind blew harder and wilder, Zeke felt a kind of settling deep in his chest.

Because this was Montana. His Montana, he often thought, though he knew better than to truly believe he had any ownership of land this untamable, this vast, this deeply wild and unknowable. He knew he was a steward at best.

Zeke was at peace with that. He had to be, or he wouldn't have managed to live here this long, much less actively encourage his children to carry that torch.

Still, Careys had lived here in these mountains for a good long while now, and Zeke understood that there was a kind of magic that happened in these hills. There always had been.

Mountains were wily things. They were never quite where you left them, and they had a way of making their wants and needs known—like it or not.

These particular mountains that spread out behind Copper Mountain liked to claim those who were part of them—like it or not. They knew who needed their brand of magic the same way they always knew who didn't.

A Montanan knew how to respect the mountains, or he wasn't much of a Montanan.

Zeke couldn't help but think that this Christmas, it was Knox's turn to find his way home at last.

Not just stay here a while longer on Zeke's deathwatch, but to sink in a few roots at last and finally figure out that he wasn't just born here, he belonged here.

That hummed in him like a Christmas carol and he knew that was the mountains' doing too.

"Make a Christmas wish," he told Belinda, smiling down at her pretty face, even prettier after all these years and the blessings of time and care. "I have a feeling it's going to come true."

She looked up at him the way she always did, her gaze filled with lightning and love, and she stretched up to wrap her arms around his neck.

"My dreams always come true, Zeke Carey," she told him, his full name like a song in her mouth. "I accept nothing less."

And then she laughed as he picked her up and swung her

into his arms, because he might have been older than should have been possible these days, and dying according to some, but he still knew how to hold his woman and carry her over to their bed.

Where they kept each other warm late into the night, when the wind picked up and the house lost power, and as far as Zeke could tell, the mountains were out there doing their wild and wintry best to bring the magic on home.

Chapter One

KNOX CAREY WAS working late when the power went out, again. He'd lost count of how many times it had gone out this week—and most of those times had been over the last few days when a nasty front moved in and squatted down over Paradise Valley. The weather had eased up the slightest bit today, but he'd known better than to imagine it was done.

This was Montana in December. Storms were only to be expected.

It had been snowing on and off for days now, blanketing the hills and making everything look like the kind of Christmas cards his mother loved to send out. Knox had the one she'd hand-delivered the day after Thanksgiving on his refrigerator—the only decoration marring the sleek steel surface.

Because a wise man didn't argue with his mother.

In fact, no one argued with Belinda Carey, because it was a lost cause.

He laughed at that. Then he rubbed his hands over his face and pushed back from the desk he'd been sitting at for far too long tonight.

Knox checked to make sure that his work was saved, something he'd always been paranoid about after growing up in this place of iffy power and capricious electricity. It had only taken one lost homework assignment when he'd been in middle school to teach him that it always paid to be that kind of paranoid.

Tonight it paid off again. He hadn't lost a thing.

He left his small, efficient office and roamed out into the main part of the house. He was proud of this house, built the farthest away from the rest of his family, down near the bottom pasture along the drive that led up to the main house. The rest of his brothers had their houses in a sort of line, though with a whole lot of space between them, on the western side of the drive. They assumed Knox had chosen the eastern side, and the closest plot to the road that led into Cowboy Point, to make a statement.

Truth was, he liked the view—but he didn't care if they assigned him all manner of darker motivations. He was the youngest of five bullheaded brothers. He liked to keep them guessing.

He'd built this house with the help of those bullheaded, mouthy, annoying brothers when he was eighteen, as was the family tradition. And he'd endured the usual complaints from them that his preferences (they'd called them demands) were *too much*.

Knox liked things the way he liked them. His only trage-dy was that he'd been raised with four older brothers who truly felt that it was their sacred duty to comment on and usually heavily critique every last thing that Knox did.

There had only been two ways to go with that, growing up. One path would have been to become a neurotic people pleaser, forever scrabbling around for approval that was unlikely to come—but that wasn't him. Knox might have been the youngest, but he was still a Carey.

He had taken the other route. The more his brothers teased him and reproached him and complained about him—usually good-naturedly, he liked to think, but still— the more set in his own opinions Knox became.

His oldest brother, Harlan, liked to call him stubborn as a mule. Knox was aware that *jackass* was the preferred term amongst the others.

But he didn't care. He'd laughed along with them and built the house he wanted.

His brothers might have built themselves rustic cabins on the pieces of property to go along with their whole Montana cowboy thing. All of them had gotten land when they were eighteen too, the better to give them their mountain men bona fides, and their cabins had reflected that. Except Ryder, who hadn't built because he'd taken off to ride bulls and live in an Airstream—a different sort of cowboy song.

Knox had always liked details. He'd always been one to slow down and see to them.

And he'd never cared for hand-me-downs or leftovers, guess why.

His house was where he'd experimented first. After building the basic structure with his brothers that first summer, he had spent years renovating the place on his own. Trying out one thing and another to see what he liked better, experimenting with different sorts of projects until he figured out what he was good at. This house was where he'd taught himself how to create properties that people wanted to live in, and better yet would pay to live in.

Thanks to this house, Knox felt confident that he could renovate anything. And he'd more than proved it.

These days he had houses he rented out in Missoula, Bigfork and Whitefish up by Flathead Lake, Bozeman, and Livingston. They all paid for themselves and made him money besides.

Something his brothers liked to laugh at around the Sunday dinner table, but every last one of them had asked him for details in private.

He could have turned on his generator to handle the dark and the cold, but when he got out into the living room he looked at the fireplace he'd made into the kind of vast hearth he'd always wanted and decided a fire would be better.

Besides, it was Christmas Eve.

His father had once told him that there were certain nights meant for contemplation, and Knox had always found that Christmas Eve was one of them.

Thinking about his father made him blow out a breath,

because he was pretty sure that the past almost two whole years had been nothing more than his family fooling themselves and sinking deep into denial. A diagnosis was a diagnosis.

No matter how healthy Zeke looked—and the old man still looked as sturdy as a mountain—he wasn't. It was a false spring hiding a killer storm. It couldn't be true.

He hated thinking that, but it was reality.

Zeke was dying.

Though Knox had made himself a solemn promise when he'd heard the news at Easter that year. He'd never intended to spend the rest of his life in Cowboy Point. It was one of the reasons he'd gone all the way to Missoula for school. He would have gone farther if it had been up to him. Not right after college, because he'd agreed to spend his twenties pitching in on the ranch. It was the least he could do, he'd thought and still thought now, because he respected what his family had built. What his father and his brothers had dedicated their lives to.

He'd wanted to make sure he was a part of that too.

But he'd been ready to try something else when his father had made that fateful, terrible announcement.

And it was tempting, now, to think that it was a miracle that the year Zeke had been given to live was coming up on two. But if there was one thing Knox had figured out over the years, it was that miracles weren't real.

Cancer didn't magically disappear. People died.

This world the Careys lived in was going to change, and probably soon, whether his family liked it or not.

It didn't exactly make him happy to think these things, but Knox had always considered himself a realist. Maybe it hit a little harder tonight, because it was Christmas Eve and he liked to think of the old man up the hill from him, still walking tall. Still working with his hands, though these days that was more for the bespoke spurs and bits he'd started selling at the Farm & Craft Market.

Still here, he thought.

Knox built the fire, aware that almost everything he knew how to do with his own hands was a direct result of his father's more weathered hands showing him the way.

It turned out he had to swallow at that, and hard.

He watched the fire as it grew and when he was satisfied, he moved away and ran through his options. Was it a whiskey sort of a night? It felt like it, but the other side of that was the fact that it was Christmas tomorrow morning— and here it was close to midnight—and his mother was definitely going to expect an appearance even if he had to snowshoe the whole way up the side of the hill. And if Belinda got the faintest *hint* of an idea that he'd indulged himself in too much whiskey or anything else tonight, she would inevitably turn to one of her time-honored traditions.

That being pounding pots and pans together to make the most noise possible, to teach her rowdy boys a lesson.

The lesson Knox had learned from watching her do such

things to his brothers was to make sure she never saw *him* hungover.

The power flickered on again then, but Knox was happy he'd made the fire because he knew better than to trust that it would stay on tonight.

There was the blustering sound of wind slamming into the side of the house, and he moved over to the front door. He peered out through the window he'd built there for exactly this purpose, but there was only snow coming down in sheets on the far side of his porch, looking relentless.

It was also looking more like a blizzard than a storm to his eye, though sometimes it was hard to tell the difference this high in the mountains.

He turned away, thinking he'd head into the kitchen to find himself something to eat and maybe dream a little bit of far-off cities that never got cold and had beaches at the ready, but stopped.

Knox didn't know why he'd stopped. But, suddenly, it was like every sense he had was on high alert.

Had he heard a sound? What sounds were there to hear out there? It wasn't just wild weather, all that howling and driving snow. It wasn't just cold and dangerous and dark, which was basically run of the mill for this part of the world at this time of year.

It was Christmas Eve. Most folks stayed home or had returned home from their merrymaking and churchgoing at this hour.

He shook it off, thinking he was imagining things—one more reason to start plotting his exit strategy again, though that was a whole lot less fun now that it was going to be predicated on a deep loss he wasn't sure he was going to recover from—

But he stopped again, and this time, he was sure he heard something.

He crossed back to the door and peered through the small window again but he couldn't see anything. He flipped on the outdoor lights, and saw what he expected to see: swirling snow coming down on the other side of his porch, and nothing but darkness beyond it.

Though something tugged at him.

Knox frowned as he realized that it looked a lot like someone or something had been out there. He couldn't think what sort of animal would be out walking around right now. Much less up onto his porch in weather like this.

Still, what he could see was that there were impressions on the stairs, like some kind of tracks.

He reached for the rifle that he kept by the door, because this was Montana and grizzlies were no joke, then pulled the door open and let the blast of the winter cold rush in.

But he hardly noticed it. Because there wasn't a grizzly bear waiting for him on the other side of the door.

There wasn't anything at all out here save what looked like the portable car seat he'd seen Harlan and Kendall carry their baby boy around in. His first thought was that they must have come down and left the baby here—because he heard, next, that little cry that must have been what had stopped him inside.

It was high-pitched, not quite a wail.

But that was ridiculous. His brother wasn't going to leave his child on a doorstep strapped into a car seat. No child should be on a doorstep in this weather.

Or at all.

Knox shot a look around the snowy, blustery dark, but he couldn't see anything or anyone else. And what must have been the footsteps of whoever had left this baby here on his porch steps were filling in rapidly, so there would be no track to follow even if he wanted to run out into the dark.

Which he couldn't do, because there was now a baby here who needed him a lot more than he needed to satisfy his curiosity.

He picked up the car seat with one hand and stepped back inside. He slammed the door behind him, then put his rifle back up on the wall where it belonged.

What Knox Carey knew about babies was pretty much zero. But he did know a thing or two about the cold in general and Montana winters in specific, and how dangerous these things were even if someone was fully grown.

He carried the car seat over to the rug laid out before the fire. Then he crouched down with it as he set it there in the heat that the fireplace threw off.

All he'd seen on the porch was a hint of a little round

cheek nestled in layers. But now, as he squatted down, he could see that those cheeks were flushed and that the baby was wrapped up in a whole lot of what looked like fleece. And that fleece was mostly pink, so Knox concluded that he was looking at a baby girl.

"Hey baby girl," he murmured, and her eyes fluttered open at the sound of his voice, then fixed on him.

Her eyes were a fascinating shade of amber-brown ringed with a darker green. Her mouth was a perfect little rosebud, and was working a little. Her cheeks were chubby and round and he thought, for some reason, that it was probably a good thing that they looked flushed instead of cold and pale.

He realized after a moment that she was wiggling in her seat, batting her arms and legs. And then that tiny little face screwed up and she let out a wail that was so loud it was more like a howl.

Knox panicked, because he had no idea what to do.

But then he thought about visiting Kendall and Harlan a couple of months ago when little baby Ezekiel James, named after his grandpa but to be known as Kiel, was brand-new. Kendall had laughed at him, told him he looked poleaxed, and said, *He's a baby, Knox. Not a poisonous snake. You know what to do with baby cows. Baby humans aren't really that different.*

So he reached in and found the straps that were keeping her in her car seat, undid them, and then picked her up. When he did, he held her before him for a moment and looked at her seriously.

She fussed and shook her arms a little like she was dancing in place in midair. And also like she was *mad*. But then she seemed to be staring right back at him.

"This is not an ideal situation," he told her gravely, and she blinked in much the same way. "We are going to have to get through this together, you and me, and it might be a little bumpy. Where is your mother?"

But of course, she was a baby, no matter how intently she seemed to be staring back at him. She didn't reply, beyond blowing a few bubbles at him.

And he couldn't stop thinking about how cold it was out there. How quickly the snow had filled in what tracks there were, which made him hope that the baby had only been out there a few minutes.

But he didn't know that for sure.

What he knew about cold exposure had nothing to do with babies specifically, but he figured it might be the same thing. Skin to skin was always the way to go, to make sure that everyone was warm and toasty and getting blood into all the extremities.

He peeled off his flannel shirt. Then he set the baby down on her back, carefully. She didn't like that very much, and started kicking and making noise. That wasn't exactly helpful when he needed to get her layers off her tiny little body, but Knox had in fact spent a lot of his life wrangling calves—as baby cows were more commonly known—and all other kinds of farm animals. Little mammals had more in common than not. He found himself murmuring soothing things, nonsensical or not, as he found her little zippers and tiny snaps and stripped the baby down until she was wearing nothing but her diaper.

A diaper he could smell, which he was pretty sure was another problem, but not one he had to deal with right this hot minute. Not yet, anyway.

He picked up the baby again, remembering what Kendall had told him about babies' heads and necks and how fragile they were, and then he nestled her into his chest. Then wrapped his shirt around her, for good measure.

And after a few moments, the little sounds she was making—of distress and protest, if he had to guess—eased.

He could feel her tiny little fingers against his skin, her little fists that had looked perfect and impossible to him. He looked down and found her staring up at him again, with those big, solemn eyes of hers, like she was taking his measure.

Knox felt something in him melt, then seem to *expand*, like his heart needed more room in his chest. He held her close, and kissed the top of her head, where there was a little tuft of reddish hair that struck him as possibly the cutest thing he'd ever beheld. She smelled soft and sweet, and he could feel the way she breathed against him with the whole of her tiny body.

He outlined what he knew about babies in his head,

which was not much. What he knew about baby animals in general was that they needed to eat and sleep a lot, and that they spent a significant portion of their young lives doing only those two things. He had no way of telling how old this baby was, but he knew that she was bigger than little new-born Kiel had been when he'd first met him. If he had to guess, she'd been born sometime in the last couple of months.

If the weather was better, he would have gone over to Kendall and Harlan's place, up the hill past the ranch house where his parents lived, to take advantage of what they'd learned since September. Or maybe not, he corrected himself, because Harlan had told everyone that Kendall and the baby had caught something and were lying low.

His next call would have been to Ryder and Rosie. Rosie had raised those twins on her own and they had more babies on the way, but of course, they were down in Marietta and as far as anyone knew, about to give birth. He could have called his parents, because they knew what to do with children of all ages, but it was just about midnight on Christmas Eve and anyway, he knew that they were taking care of Levi and Eli.

Wilder and Boone were probably the closest to him, but what did either one of them know about babies? Neither one of their wives had one. Knox figured they'd know pretty much what he did. Not much more than they could rustle up with an internet search.

That did not feel sufficient.

If this was the middle of summer, he probably would have taken the baby straight down into Marietta to have her checked out, because what if she was sick? What if she'd been sitting out there for too long and something had happened to her that he couldn't see?

The moment he thought that, he had another thought, and had to blow out a breath when it took hold.

Because he knew that it was too dangerous to drive down Copper Mountain in the middle of the night with a snowstorm pounding its way over Paradise Valley. He'd grown up here on the far side of Cowboy Point, a tiny village hidden away behind Copper Mountain that didn't have much in the way of services. Especially not this time of year. Folks around here often had to take things into their own hands medically, because no one was coming to save them. There was no calling 911 and thinking an ambulance was going to show up.

There was no getting anywhere in this weather without a truck with a tough four-wheel-drive and the determination to make it where he needed to go for the baby's sake. Knox had both.

And there was only one place that he could go that didn't involve skidding off the side of Copper Mountain like too many people did every winter.

But that was complicated.

Knox kept the baby tight against his chest as he got to his

feet, then walked back down the hall to his office to find his phone. He swiped it open, scrolled through, and then stopped when he found the name he was looking for.

But he didn't connect the call.

He could feel himself tense, everywhere, but then the baby moved in his arms and he reminded himself that this wasn't about him.

It didn't matter how complicated this was, because it didn't have anything to do with him, personally, or the past year and a half.

But because that wouldn't necessarily be obvious if he called this number, he swiped over to the internet instead, found the business number and connected that call.

It rang twice, and when she picked up, Knox braced himself.

"It's Christmas Eve, Knox," came her voice. As cool as ever. He had to close his eyes. "And I'm pretty sure I told you not to call me again."

"I'm calling the clinic," he managed to say, somehow keeping his voice even when that had never been something he was good at around this woman. "I have a situation, Doctor. And I need your help."

Chapter Two

D<small>R. RAMONA TAYLOR</small> had vowed to herself that she would never fall for Knox Carey again.

She had broken this vow numerous times before, so many times that she'd often despaired of herself, but this time she'd meant it. This time, she'd gone cold turkey.

And she'd actually kept herself clean for going on two months now.

Ramona was proud of herself for that. She'd spent a year and a half caught in the push and pull that was Knox, and the truth was, she was bruised. Emotionally battered and raw straight through. She needed, desperately, to really and truly be done with this maddeningly unavailable cowboy who'd stolen her heart at first glance, turned her inside out with a touch, and had made her cry into her lonely pillow too many times to count thereafter.

It was embarrassing. It was heartbreaking. There wasn't enough Taylor Swift in the world to handle it.

But this time she'd believed that she was finished.

This time she was really and truly moving on—she'd even started *actually dating*, because it wasn't like she was going to meet someone better for her poor heart while sitting alone in her house.

She was doing everything right, at last.

So the last thing in the world she should have been doing *right now* was driving out to his house.

Especially in this weather, she thought, as she inched her way over the hill on the far side of the small valley that made up Cowboy Point. The local Stark family's lodge was a kind of beacon at the top of that hill, the grand old Cowboy Point Lodge that they were restoring to its former glory, starting with the cottages they'd renovated and opened for business this fall. One of them was the only bookstore in the community, which made Ramona happy—though not at the moment.

There were lights beaming out into the dark through the driving snow, some of them jolly Christmas lights, but Ramona couldn't get too excited about them. Because she knew that the rest of the drive to Knox's house on his family's ranch would be dark. Entirely without light, and on questionable mountain roads.

Good thing, then, that she knew this particular drive of shame like the back of her hand.

He had told her that he would bring the baby to her, but she had refused.

We don't want to expose her to the elements again, she'd said, grateful for all the hours she'd spent perfecting her clinical manner. It was an excellent defense not only against Knox Carey himself, but against her own treacherous and traitorous heart. *I'm perfectly capable of driving out there to examine her.*

I don't know that you are, he'd replied.

She hated everything about him, Ramona told herself as she remembered the way he'd said that. That unbearably confident drawl of his, low and husky even in the middle of the night.

Or maybe what she meant was, especially in the middle of the night.

Ramona hated the way it wound itself around her neck like some kind of smoke, but not the sort that made her cough. That would have been helpful. That might have been some kind of protection against it.

The kind of smoke Knox created did nothing but kick up fires inside of her that only he could put out.

And she already knew where that led.

"No," she told herself now, leaving the lights of Cowboy Point Lodge behind and driving carefully into the snowy dark, her hands gripping the wheel of her truck so tightly that her knuckles ached. But she didn't loosen her grip. "You will not slip into old patterns of thinking. He does not *put out* any fires. He *is* a trash fire all his own, and that's all you need to know about him."

But that was not all she knew about Knox Carey. That was the problem.

I will gather some supplies and make my way to your house, she had told him coolly on the phone. She'd already jackknifed up from her bed, and had been frowning around her room, trying to decide what to wear out into all that weather at this time of night. Meanwhile, the other half of her brain had been cataloging what infant supplies she had in the clinic because she was certain Knox didn't have anything on hand.

Ramona. He'd said her name. That was all.

And it wasn't fair, of course. Her name in his mouth like that, like they were intimate. Like they were still the kind of intimate they'd been only two months ago—

Anyway, he needed to call her *doctor* now, she'd thought then. For everyone's safety. But she couldn't tell him that without giving herself away and God knew, she'd done enough of that with this man.

So she'd said nothing, angrily pulling on her long johns as she'd clamped her cell phone between her shoulder and the side of her face.

You're not from here, he'd been saying. *You don't know how to handle snow like this. Particularly not in the middle of the night.*

You don't know how to handle a baby, she retorted. *So I'm going to hang up, gather my supplies, and come see how that baby is doing. I don't know how long it will take me. If I'm not there by morning, I would appreciate you calling 911.*

She'd hung up. Because that was safer.

Now she was all alone in her truck, doing her best not to drive off the side of the Gallatin Range, or lodge herself in a gorge, not to be discovered until the spring melt at the earliest. She'd been worried that she might fall asleep on the way, but it hadn't taken her more than a couple of minutes of navigating her way out of her own driveway to realize that wasn't going to be a problem.

Because this was terrifying. Her adrenaline was kicking at her. Hard.

The fact that she had driven this road a million times should have helped, but it didn't. The snow made everything bewildering, and scary. She'd grown up in New Hampshire, which was certainly snowy and wintry enough to call itself the northern state it was, but it was nothing like this.

Still, she knew enough to keep driving slowly, the whole world narrowing down to the distance between one pole stuck in the drifts to mark the side of the road, and also to mark the level of snowfall, and the next.

Ramona knew that eventually, this road ended up at High Mountain Ranch. And after that, it was a relatively short shot to Knox's house. Just up the main drive past the first pasture, down the first offshoot that wasn't really a road, and then there sat his house on the right.

She just had to trust that this would happen. She had to trust that no matter how strange and otherworldly everything looked, and how much longer it all seemed to take, she was moving in the right direction and would get where she needed to go. Eventually.

In the meantime, she thought about how grateful she was for this truck. When she had decided to move out here, all the way into a middle of nowhere Montana town that none of her friends in Chicago could believe she would consider, she had tried to be as practical as possible. Because there was a lot of sentimentality in moving into her grandfather's old house. There was nothing but emotion as far as that was concerned.

But if she wanted to really *live* in that house, and work there, it would require practicality.

Her grandfather had been a blustery, laconic, gruff old man who Ramona had loved to distraction. He had been her mother's father and Ramona had spent her summers out here with him, riding horses in the mountains and listening to him complain endlessly about how built-up everything was getting, here in a place where they could go days without seeing another person unless they wanted to.

He had done ranch work his whole life and in his old age, with aching bones, he'd settled into part-time work at the feed store in Cowboy Point and a whole lot of storytelling with the other old-timers out in front of the diner that was connected to the General Store. He had never married again once he'd put his beloved Isabella into her grave down in the churchyard along the creek. He'd had his own name carved next to hers, so there could be no doubt about where he was headed.

Ramona's mother found him impossible, too hardheaded, too set in his ways, too obstinate. She had tried to get him to move out east to be closer to her, but he'd always refused.

He had died when Ramona was in college, and she'd known by then what she'd wanted to do. She'd known it since she was a kid and her grandfather had told her stories about things like water rights in the West, the trouble rural communities had living so far away from everything, and how painful it was to have to make the choice between living the way they wanted to live—wild and free beneath the great big sky—or clustered in somewhere surrounded by other people because that was where things like hospitals were.

Didn't rightly seem fair, to her grandpa's way of thinking.

He'd left her his house, which her mother claimed he'd done simply to be spiteful. Because he'd known, Bettina Taylor claimed, that *she* would obviously have sold it off and freed the family from its Montana fever, and he was an ornery old man who'd written off his only daughter when she'd moved away.

Or, Mom, Ramona had said—more than once, *he knew that* I *loved it there.*

Don't be silly, Bettina had always replied. *It's a wide spot in a forgotten road. Nobody loves it there.*

Needless to say, Bettina had not been remotely supportive when Ramona had told her that she was moving back to Bettina's hometown. Not for the summer, but for good.

But you're a doctor, Bettina had said, staring at Ramona without comprehension. *You could live anywhere. Why on earth would you go back there?*

You do know that not everybody hates Montana as much as you do, right? Ramona had replied, with a lot less patience than when she had been a college student. Or maybe she just didn't feel the need to be quite as careful any longer, as a grown-up *doctor* and all. *It's actually a famous and beloved tourist destination. And Cowboy Point isn't the town you grew up in. You haven't been back in what? Thirty years?*

Either way, it's a waste of your talent, her mother had said. With a certain stubbornness Ramona had reluctantly come to realize was a family trait.

That's where you're wrong, Ramona had told her. Calmly. *It's exactly what I've always wanted to focus my talent on. I'm opening a clinic. I'm going to take care of the community Grandpa loved. I think he'd be pleased.*

Of course he would be pleased, her mother had shot back at her. *He was always pleased when he got his own way.* But then she had hugged Ramona, fiercely. *I'm sure you'll be the brightest light that town has ever seen.*

Ramona didn't know about that. But what she didn't want was to become a cautionary tale about out-of-staters who came into Montana and had no idea what they were doing. So she had picked her mother's brain and done significant research before she'd moved. After her years in Chicago, she felt pretty sure that she could handle the winters, but she hadn't lived in a *rural* area in Chicago, obviously. That was the difference. She was used to the cold, and the snow, but she wasn't responsible for clearing any of it or getting around in it when it wasn't cleared.

The truck had been her first major Montana purchase. She needed it to be a kind of tank that could get her anywhere, through any kind of weather, and that she could sleep in if she had to. That was something she'd tested out when she'd driven out from Chicago.

She'd known that she would also need the truck to be a kind of clinic on wheels, especially when she did house calls, and it was. Even at the height of summer, she would still be contending with the Rocky Mountains in all their glory and it always was wise to have a healthy respect for what mountains might bring to any situation.

Ramona had more than enough respect. Especially with her truck. She had moved out one June and had set about renovating the house. She'd had it all planned out in advance, and had talked to all the necessary people and institutions to make it happen. She wanted to set herself up as a clinic, making it so folks didn't have to go skidding down that terrifying road into Marietta when they were already hurt or sick. That was her first priority.

But she'd also wanted to find her own place in the community her grandfather had left behind. Ramona had figured that it wouldn't be *too* hard to make friends because she'd always been good at that, and she hadn't been wrong on that score. There were all kinds of interesting people in Cowboy Point. She'd found Cat Lisle—now Cat Carey—at the pizza place purely by chance. Now she couldn't imagine running the clinic without her. She, Cat, and the Carey wife who had once been a Stark, Rosie, spent a lot of time together. She'd also started becoming friends with the latest Carey family addition by marriage, Sierra Tate.

Her goal for the new year coming in fast was to spend less time with members of the Carey family. Because as much as she liked her friends, it really wasn't any good for her mental health. Proximity to Knox made her do stupid things.

Ramona was very tired of being stupid.

The conventional wisdom was that folks who moved to Montana in the summer suffered through one winter and slunk off back to where they came from because they couldn't take it. It was true. Ramona had seen a significant uptick in friendliness when she'd made it through her first winter.

You must be done with this experiment by now, her mother had said when they'd talked, earlier today. Or yesterday, Ramona corrected herself, looking at the clock on her dashboard that read 1:56 in the morning. *It's been a smashing success, and who could be surprised? It's you. You make all of these uphill battles look easy. But surely it's time to come home.*

Ramona hadn't thought through her response. *I am home,* she had told her mother.

That had not gone over well.

Now, out here in this treacherous dark—inching along the road that was more of a suggestion she held in the back of her mind than any actual passageway—she had time to think that through.

And the truth was, it did feel like home. Finally, she'd found her way home.

The only fly in all that ointment was Knox.

Because Ramona had met him on her very first night as a Montana resident.

She had driven up Copper Mountain, and parked the truck she now knew that she could live in for weeks at a time, if necessary, behind her grandfather's old house. She'd spent most of the afternoon caught between nostalgia and overwhelm. Because while it was a delight to be back in the place that she had loved so much as a girl, it also wasn't the same place she remembered. It had been left to its own devices for far too long.

She had walked around the property, set back from the main road that led into the little community of Cowboy Point, near where the tiny local library stood. There was a falling down shed out back, but the house itself was sturdy. She had already figured out the layout in her head and how she would turn the ground floor into a clinic with her own living area upstairs. Maybe one day she'd renovate the shed, too.

All of those dreams had seemed doable on the drive out here, across the Midwest and through the grasslands and the rolling plains. But once she'd actually arrived, she'd found that she questioned her ability to do any of it.

So she'd taken a long shower and had walked into town

to see if there was any food to be had on that first, bright June evening.

She had found Mountain Mama Pizza bustling, with a band out on the patio beneath strings of happy lights. She'd gotten herself a beer and one of their special pizzas, and even though she hadn't known a single soul in that restaurant that night, she had felt her optimism rising again.

Because it felt like the kind of place she wanted to call her own. It felt like the Cowboy Point she remembered from her summers with her grandfather. He had known everyone in town, just as all those people that night had seemed to know each other. It was different from the town she had grown up in back in New Hampshire that was far more manicured and tailored to the fancy college that was at the center of all life there. They kept the wilderness to the White Mountains in the north and pretty photographs of the snow when it fell in town.

Cowboy Point felt more genuine to her, somehow. Maybe that was why she'd liked it so much all along.

She had finished eating and had been enjoying a second beer when Knox had walked by her table and smiled at her.

And Ramona had debated this a lot, looking back.

Had it been that moment? Had it been as simple as that smile? Or the way he'd stopped still as if he'd hit an invisible wall, and could do nothing at all but stare at her?

She had certainly felt the electricity between them. It should have been shocking—but the way he smiled made it feel more like honey all through her body.

Not less shocking, but sweeter.

"Why don't I know you?" he had asked, and that smile of his had made what should have been a clichéd sort of line feel new, real, and breathless. "Please tell me who you are so we can rectify that as soon as possible."

He had sat down with her at that table and that had been the beginning of it all.

Since then, everything between them had been that same explosive, electric conflagration, too sweet and too hot to bear, and time hadn't dulled it at all.

Over the past year and a half, there had been times when she'd thought that it might work out. When he'd spent every night in her bed, or she'd been a fixture in his, and she had been certain that it all had to *mean* something.

But it never did.

Or, if she was brutally honest with herself, it had never meant what she *wanted* it to mean.

And she had come to the reluctant, painful conclusion that if she wanted the life she'd always dreamed about having here, she needed to insist on more.

So she had.

And Knox Carey had declined the offer to step into that kind of intensity. Or anything that hinted at something permanent. It was a line he refused to cross.

That, of course, really should have been the end of it. To her enduring shame, it wasn't. The end had come much later, after months and months of heartache and hooking up and hurting herself with her own feelings again and again and again.

Now here they were, having not interacted at all in two months, which was a record. And even though she was driving to his house in the middle of the night—not exactly a new thing in their tortured little story—Ramona reminded herself that this was not a booty call.

There was a baby in the mix. In case she had been tempted to think he was making that up, she'd heard the unmistakable sounds of an infant through the phone.

Ramona would like to believe that she wouldn't have gone if she hadn't heard those sounds, having moved on and all, but she wasn't sure that was true—and that was lowering. Extremely lowering.

Up before her in the middle of the swirling snow, she saw the tall posts she was looking for loom up out of the dark. And up on top, the wooden sign that read *High Mountain Ranch*.

Ramona felt relief wash all through her, though she wouldn't have admitted it if anyone asked. Especially if that anyone was Knox.

But part of her really had thought that she'd driven off into the unmarked part of the mountains, where it was entirely possible that she would have been lost forever.

People off in more civilized places couldn't possibly understand what the true Montana wilderness was really like.

They drove through the national parks on paved roads and marveled at the views and never left the safety of their vehicles to test themselves against the true splendor of the West.

Much less the other side of that splendor, which was its majestic power, and all the many ways it could kill... everything.

Ramona let her grip on the steering wheel relax a bit, because feeling small in Montana made her happy. It was why she moved here. And some part of her thought that was why she could pull off drives like this—but she was still ecstatic that she'd made it to the ranch. She blew out a long, shuddering sort of breath as she turned in at the sign.

She accepted the fact that she really hadn't thought she was going to make it, shuddered, and let it go.

Because now, even if she spun off into a ditch, she would be on Carey property. If absolutely necessary, she could walk to safety. And if for some reason she couldn't make it out of the vehicle, she knew one of the Careys would find her.

It was amazing what a difference that made. On a physical level inside of her.

That was one more thing she was never going to admit to any Montana natives, no matter how much she liked feeling small here.

The road into the ranch was piled high with snow, but it was easier to find her way because the drive was cut through the overhanging trees and there were no cliffs on either side.

This meant she could inch along until she got the first gap in the trees on the right side, which she knew was the way to Knox's house.

And then, after she bumped that way a while, careful to stay between the lines of forest on both sides all heavy with snow, she saw lights.

This was the best yet because she knew they would lead straight up to that house of his. It was a kind of modern farmhouse, though he'd stepped back on the black shutter thing that seemed to be ubiquitous these days. Ramona knew perfectly well that it was a beautiful house, objectively speaking. Not everyone could live in a haunted house. She might consider Knox's farmhouse a little bit soulless, personally, but that's what he liked.

Or that's what he claimed to like.

Because Knox Carey was charming. Everyone agreed. But at the first hint of anything like a feeling?

He was gone.

Ramona felt this was reflected in the house he'd built here and lived in like it was a hotel.

"None of that is your business," she muttered to herself as she drew near. "And none of it matters tonight anyway."

She pulled up as close to his porch as she could. And turned off the truck, then took a moment to collect herself, because she was pretty sure that drive would feature prominently in her nightmares for some time. But that time was not now. Now she had to get her doctor game face on.

Ramona grabbed her medical bag and the backpack she'd stuffed full of infant supplies, then climbed out of the truck, not surprised to find herself in snow up to her thighs.

She waded through it—inelegantly—and then fought her way up onto the porch where she stamped her feet. Loudly. Trying to knock the snow off, but also alerting Knox that she had arrived.

By the time she made it to the front door, it was opening.

Then she had to stop and stare, as always, because she was here to do her doctor thing but she was only a girl. Especially around him.

Knox filled the doorway, and it wasn't fair. *He* wasn't fair, on any level.

His dark hair was a mess, but that in no way detracted from the painfully masculine beauty of his face. He was far too good-looking. That had always been true.

Tonight he looked a little bit frazzled, but, of course, he made that kind of hot. His eyes looked sleepy and they were that bright golden color that told her he was *feeling things*, which he never liked. He had an impossible jaw line that was covered in stubble this late, and she knew exactly how it felt to take that face of his in her hands and kiss his mouth until she felt dizzy.

He was also bare chested, which would normally send very different signals. Since he was all hard planes and ridges of abdominal muscles, and favored battered jeans that rode low on his hips, and usually had a particular heat in his gaze when he answered the door like that.

Ramona had spent a lot of time bemoaning the fact that any man could look *this* good.

But tonight he was also cradling a tiny, chubby baby in his arms, which did damage to her in ways she wasn't sure she was going to recover from. Possibly ever. Because she'd dreamed about moments like this. Knox and a baby.

She'd learned better than to let those dreams linger and now here they were—

When she stood there and stared, he scowled at her.

"I don't want her to catch a chill," he told her gruffly.

Ramona stamped her way inside, closed the door behind her, and tried to get her bearings.

Normally when she arrived on his doorstep, he met her at the door—but not like this. It was usually a fight or a surrender, or both, and they usually ended up naked. Sometimes right there on the floor in what was essentially his foyer in all this open space he liked.

She couldn't say she was proud of that, but it was in the past.

And everything was different tonight, obviously.

You need to get your head in the game, she told herself, the way her grandpa would have.

Ramona put down her supplies and then set about stripping off her outer layers. It was always a production. She pulled off her boots and her cold weather gear, then placed it neatly on the bench next to the door that existed for exactly that purpose. She hung her coat on one of the pegs on the wall, and tugged off her hat and scarf and shoved them into one sleeve.

When she turned back around to face him, he was watching her much too closely.

She pretended she didn't notice.

"Let's see what we're dealing with here with this little sweetheart," Ramona said, in her best clinical voice.

She motioned for him to follow her as she marched herself into his kitchen, where she knew his counters would be clean and gleaming. They were. She set her medical bag on one end, and then held out her hands.

Something inside of her seemed to shift precipitously when Knox looked alarmed. And reluctant. Like he didn't want to let go of the child.

"I'm not going to hurt her," Ramona assured him, though her throat was suddenly tight. "I need to examine her."

"Right, of course," he muttered.

But it still seemed to take him a minute to pull the baby off his chest and let Ramona take her from him.

She cuddled the baby close and cooed at her, tracking the baby's responses. Ramona held her close as she moved over to the drawer where she knew Knox kept kitchen towels that were happily oversized and always clean, and she spread a couple of them out over the cold counter. Then she set the baby down on them, murmuring to the little girl as she did it.

Then she conducted a full exam, culminating in a diaper change. When she was done, she put the baby on her hip and prepared a bottle, noting how greedy the little girl seemed when she started to suck it down.

Only then did she allow herself to pay closer attention to Knox, who had shrugged into a T-shirt at some point and was watching her intently.

"She seems perfectly healthy, even happy," Ramona told him, smiling because babies always made her smile. She remembered who she was talking to and dialed it back. "It's a miracle. Do you know how long she was left outside?"

"I don't think it could have been long," Knox said, frowning. "I could still see footsteps in the snow, but you saw how hard it was coming down. Tracks can't have lasted long out there."

"Well, she came through her ordeal like a champ," Ramona said. She looked up at him, and it was a fight to keep her voice cool, but she managed it. Somehow, she managed it. "Have you given any thought to who might have left her here?"

"A maniac?" he retorted.

"You haven't really thought this through, have you?" Ramona asked, and again, it was painful to keep her voice calm. But a suspicion had taken her over while she was examining the child and she couldn't let it go. "There's only one reason that someone would leave a baby here, don't you think? One very obvious reason."

Knox looked at her like she was speaking in tongues. "I can't think of any reason that someone would leave a baby here."

"That's actually my point." Ramona said this quietly, because her heart was doing wild things in her chest and she wasn't sure she was breathing, either. "There are all kinds of reasons that women abandon their babies, and they're usually very sad. Still, normally, they do it in places where they know the baby will be found and cared for. Hospitals. Police stations. Firehouses. Why would anyone drive up here in this kind of weather? I'll tell you, it was pretty horrific out there."

He stared back at her, something like a scowl on his face, as he braced himself against the counter across from her. "I don't know where you're going with this."

"Why would a woman drive up and leave her baby on the doorstep of a man who has exhibited no sign whatsoever, ever as far as I know, of being capable of or interested in taking care of a child?" She didn't keep that as calm as she should have. "Take a wild guess, Knox."

"Just because I've never taken care of a child doesn't mean that I'd be *incapable* of it," he shot back.

Like that was the point of this.

"You're not exactly known as the Mr. Rogers of Cowboy Point, are you?" She shook her head at him, aware that there was something trembling deep inside of her. Maybe a scream. Maybe, worse, a sob. "So why would someone do this?"

"It seems pretty clear to me you have an answer to that, Ramona." His gaze was gold and hot and clearly furious. "So why don't you just tell me."

She made herself smile, professionally.

Even though it hurt.

"I think it's pretty clear all on its own," she said.

"Not to me," he shot back. "But by all means, keep being cryptic in the middle of the night with an abandoned, motherless baby in your arms. That feels like the right path to take."

Ramona looked down at the little girl, whose eyes were closed as she busily sucked on her bottle. Then she looked back at this man who had ruined her life in too many ways to count—or maybe she'd ruined it herself, because of him, but the end result was still the same—and wished just for one moment he couldn't be *quite so* tragically beautiful.

But this was the price of that beauty, wasn't it? Babies on doorsteps and a sea of broken hearts.

Not to mention all that bright gold heat in his gaze when he was busy showing her, once again, that she was the only person alive in all the world that he was *not* charming for.

She'd thought that meant something too. Now she suspected it was just that he was an asshole, and surely tonight proved that beyond any shadow of a doubt.

"I didn't realize it would be hard to follow," she told him, and kept that smile on her face because she could be an asshole too. "Come on, Knox. She's obviously yours."

Chapter Three

I F THE GOOD doctor had taken a baseball bat to the side of his head, Knox couldn't have been more shocked.

"Mine?" He couldn't make sense of that. "What do you mean, *mine?*"

Ramona was doing her calm, cool, collected thing, but he could see something a lot sharper and brighter in those blue eyes of hers. "What do you think that term normally means, Knox?" She looked down at the baby. "You're obviously the father of this child."

"No." He threw that out, flat and sure. "I'm not."

Ramona only gazed at him, something too frigid for his peace of mind in her gaze. "I'd estimate that she's two months old. So if we count back, what you need to ask yourself is who you were sleeping with last winter."

He found that he was gripping the countertop so hard that he couldn't tell if he was going to break off a chunk of it or break his own fingers. Both were appealing options just then.

"You know who I was sleeping with last winter," he gritted out.

The way she shrugged made him feel something like apoplectic, but he tamped it down.

Even when she smiled in a way that made him feel scrubbed raw. "As you made sure to point out to me on approximately ten thousand different occasions, we never had any claim to each other. But here is this baby. Pretty much all the claim necessary to *someone*, I'd say."

"Ramona. She's not my child."

She moved toward him and Knox didn't know what he thought she would do, but when Ramona handed over the baby he took her, like it was an automatic response.

"In the absence of any evidence to the contrary, we'll have to assume that she is." He thought she looked murderous, and it was a problem that something in him found that thrilling, because it was so damn hard to get beneath her surface. But she wasn't done. "Again, why else would someone leave her here, in the middle of a blizzard, on Christmas Eve?"

"I don't know," he replied. He adjusted the soft, warm weight of the baby in his arms. "But I can tell you right now, it's not because I'm the father."

Though even as he said that, he could understand why she thought otherwise. Because really. What other reason could there be? It wasn't like he was a kindergarten teacher. Or a doctor like Ramona.

He was never going to be anyone's first choice as a babysitter, much less a whole parent.

None of this made sense.

The baby in his arms fidgeted, and he adjusted the way he was holding her to give her better access to the bottle that Ramona had prepared. She blinked open her eyes and looked at him, and it was like he couldn't help himself. It was like he was falling forward into her gaze, it was so solemn and intent. He made a low, humming sound, that seemed to please her, so he did it again.

It wasn't that he forgot Ramona was there—he was always entirely too aware of where Ramona Taylor was, to everyone's detriment—but it took him a moment to look over at her again. When he did, she was watching him with a look he couldn't read on her face.

That was also nothing new. He took the baby and went over to his favorite chair in this room, an oversized armchair that turned out to be an excellent place to hold a tiny little football of a baby who gave off enough heat to rival his fireplace and was a sweet little deadweight in his arms.

Ramona stayed where she was, her arms crossed over her chest and all her usual shields in place. He told himself he shouldn't care. That this was none of his business. He'd made sure of that, hadn't he?

The only noise was a crackle of the fire and the baby's intense sucking.

It was the middle of the night, and he was perfectly aware that this was the only time Ramona had been in his house this long and had kept all of her clothes on.

And he knew every single reason that they couldn't work

out, but that had never helped him much. It didn't help him now.

Because Ramona was, very simply, the most compelling woman he'd ever seen in his life.

He could still remember the first moment he'd seen her because it was burned into his brain. He hadn't seen her walk into the pizza place that night, but he had certainly seen her when he'd walked through the big, main room on his way toward the patio where a band had been playing. It had been like walking face first into a wall. He couldn't remember what he'd said. Knox had only managed to focus on her smile.

She was slender and lean, but strong. She liked to run on the trails around town, weather permitting. She liked to hike, too, and walked into town whenever she could rather than driving, though it was about a mile. That was the kind of energy she always had even when she was sitting still, or tending to her patients, or driving him wild in bed.

There was an intensity about Ramona Taylor that called to Knox in ways he couldn't explain. If he'd had to put together a list of things that comprised his dream woman, it would have been... just Ramona.

She was smart. She was quick, funny, decisive. She had the kind of face that belonged in art museums, or those lockets with pictures inside them. Her eyes were so blue that it was impossible not to compare them to the sky—that wild blue Montana sky that stretched into eternity. Ramona had straight, golden-blond hair that she was always twisting back out of her way, or putting into sleek ponytails, and he liked to get his hands in the thick silk of it, make it messy, and make it *his*.

Knox had never been a saint, but there was something about the way he and Ramona fit together that he couldn't let himself think about too closely now. Not with the baby in his arms, because the last thing he needed to do was get too worked up.

The last time she'd left him, she'd been pretty clear that she was done with him.

He'd agreed that was the right decision, and had then downed a bottle of whiskey and sat right here in this chair until he couldn't sit upright. Not his finest hour.

Not something he intended to share with her, either.

That first night, though, he'd walked her home to Old Man Dade's place and she'd let him in, then had shared the single bottle of wine she had on the premises. She'd told him very seriously that she absolutely did not sleep with a man on the first day she met him.

So when it was after midnight and technically not the same day, Knox pulled her to him and kissed her like he meant it to last forever. And they'd discovered exactly how well they could come together right there on the floor of that old house he'd thought was haunted when he was a kid.

Now it felt like the house was haunting him every time he drove past.

She was the perfect woman. There was no denying it. But she was very open about the fact that she'd come to Cowboy Point to put down roots. To stay.

And Knox had always known that he was leaving.

If he'd been the good man he'd always wished he was, he wouldn't have walked her home. He wouldn't have stopped at her table. He wouldn't have let the impossible electric charge that sparked so bright between them muddy the waters.

If he had been a better man, he wouldn't have started any of this.

But if he'd been any kind of virtuous, he wouldn't know how she tasted. He wouldn't know how perfectly those long legs of hers could wrap around his hips, or the truly amazing things she could do with her mouth.

And despite everything, Knox thought even now, that would be a crying shame.

Her gaze narrowed as she watched him, and he got the impression that she knew everything he was thinking. Her mouth firmed, which didn't help the direction of his thoughts, but she walked farther into the big living space.

She did not come over to him in his chair. She went over to the car seat instead and knelt down beside it, frowning.

"What are you doing?" he asked.

"Looking for some clue as to who this little love really is," Ramona said. She didn't look at him while she said it.

The baby was still working on her bottle, so Knox

watched, feeling a little upended himself as Ramona examined the discarded, bright pink fleecy items that Knox had taken off the little girl when he'd worried she needed warming.

Ramona folded everything and put the fuzzy pink hat on top. Then she pulled the blankets out of the well of the seat and made a little noise of triumph. She looked over at him as she lifted out what looked like a pack of papers shoved into a Ziploc bag from the bottom of the car seat.

"Look at that," Ramona said, waving the packet. "Clues." But she didn't pry open the plastic bag. She only looked at him. "I'm not sure you want me rifling through your daughter's private things."

"You can look at whatever you want," Knox replied, and he was proud of the way he kept his voice even, even though he knew this couldn't be his daughter. "I have nothing to hide."

He could read her expression then, which probably meant she wanted him to, and it was skeptical. Down to the bone skeptical.

And the thing about Ramona, Knox knew, was that this was his fault. All of it. He knew that. He had always prided himself on being direct. Honest no matter what.

That way, whatever happened, there might be some emotions but there could be no real surprises.

It had always served him well.

Maybe that was why he'd never known how to tell Ramona that she was a greater temptation than any he'd faced before. She wasn't like anyone else. He had always told her the truth. Every time.

Trouble was, the truth for him kept changing.

He'd accepted a while ago that any way he looked at it, he came out the dick in this scenario. That didn't make him happy, but he couldn't see any way to change it, either.

It seemed to take her a minute to jerk her gaze away from his. Then she opened the plastic bag and pulled out what was inside. And for a long moment, she was quiet as she read what was in front of her, shuffled the pages, then read more.

"What does it say?" Knox asked.

Ramona looked over at him, her face suspiciously blank. He knew that served her well in the work she did, but he'd never liked it aimed at him.

He liked it even less tonight.

She went and put the papers on his coffee table, and then took the baby from him. She kissed the tiny girl on her forehead, taking the bottle away and then shifting the baby to her shoulder. He watched her do this with an expert ease, not entirely sure why that, too, made that familiar hunger inside of him grow bigger. With fangs.

Ramona went back into the kitchen and rummaged around in the bag she'd brought, then tossed a soft towel over one shoulder. Knox watched, still mesmerized, as Ramona began to jiggle the baby on that shoulder, tapping gently on her tiny back and rubbing it in small circles.

She caught his eyes on her and her gaze darkened. "She needs to be burped before we put her down to sleep."

They both seemed to hear that *we* in the same moment, and it clearly hit both of them the same way, Knox thought. He was sure he saw Ramona flinch a little bit.

And as for him, there was something about all of this that was hitting him the *wrong* way.

Or hitting him too hard, maybe.

Either way, it was hard to get his bearings, so he turned his attention to the packet of papers Ramona had left on the table. The first one looked like a timetable, and after frowning at it he realized it was a feeding schedule. When the baby ate, how much, and then how and when she slept. Straightforward enough.

The next took a minute to figure out, but he was pretty sure it was a vaccination schedule, indicating which ones the baby had already gotten and which ones she was still set to receive. All good.

But the third page stopped him cold. Like a stake through the heart.

Because it was a photocopy of a birth certificate. The date of said birth was October 24. Exactly two months ago. But Knox didn't have time to be impressed with how Ramona had nailed the baby's age, because he was too busy looking at the rest of the information on this document.

Where it said mother's name, it said *Shoshana Delaney.* A name he'd never heard in his entire life.

The baby's name was what made his heart start to kick hard in his chest. The baby's name was recorded as *Hailey*. That was fine. Cute, even.

But the last name was listed as *Carey*.

And on the line for the father, he read his own name.

For a moment it was like everything went blank.

When he could access his brain again, he counted back from October 24. But no matter how many times he did it, he came up with the same result.

The reality was that there were times in his life where he would have had more cause to worry that something like this was real. More cause to be concerned that a condom had broken without his knowledge, or something else had happened to make it less effective. No matter how careful a person was, it was always a risk.

But that didn't hold true for this past winter.

"I have no earthly idea who Shoshana Delaney is," Knox said, his voice low, and not really sounding much like his own.

"That makes it even better," Ramona replied with a small laugh that wasn't exactly filled with merriment. Knox couldn't even look over at her. She cleared her throat and looked at him with a kind of weaponized *politeness*. "Well, Knox, how many nights do you think you had with strange women whose names you never got? Maybe we can work backwards from there. Can you pick out any identifying features from your memories? Were there any personality traits that might help you differentiate between them?"

And it had been a long night already. Knox had gone from contemplating a quiet whiskey on a holiday night to caring for a two-month-old baby in an instant and he wasn't sure he was handling the transition well. He had no idea what would happen next. And he had a copy of the baby's birth certificate with his name on it.

It was one sucker punch after the next.

But this one left his head spinning.

For a moment, he felt paralyzed. He was frozen there in that chair in a state of sheer disbelief.

He watched as Ramona came over to the couch. She set the baby down and then piled pillows all around her so there was no possible way she could fall off the couch.

And he realized that she had a tell, his ice cold doctor. He could see it in the way she moved, that humming tension in her limbs. He'd begun to think she really was unreadable.

But that didn't really help him any just now.

He cleared his throat and it took effort. "I just want to be clear about what you're accusing me of here."

"I'm not accusing you of anything," she shot back at him. "You've lived your life as you've seen fit and I have no opinion on it."

"You clearly have an opinion on it, Ramona."

"You made it clear that I was not allowed to have an opinion on it," she threw at him, and he thought he saw a glimmer of hurt in all of that blue.

He sat forward in the chair, resting his elbows on his knees and clasping his hands together, because it was that or he thought he might put a fist through a wall. And that was hardly the kind of man he aspired to be. Or had ever been before.

"This birth certificate is a lie," he told her, very deliberately. Very intently. "And I'll tell you how I know that, Ramona," he continued when she made a scoffing sound. "I don't have to think about identifying marks or standout personalities in some drunken haze. It never happened. I haven't actually slept with anyone but you since the day I met you."

She straightened as if she'd sustained a body blow and her gaze snapped to his. With something like alarm, he thought.

"You don't have to tell these stories," she said, her voice low and even more hurt, to his ear. He hated it. "I don't have anything to do with this."

He couldn't tell why that bothered him so much, but it did.

"I've had fun," Knox bit out. He didn't mean to get to his feet, but then there he was, standing. "I'd like to think that anyone who was with me had fun too. And if during that time in my life someone had come along and put a birth certificate like this in my face I would have had to go take a DNA test to be sure." He pinned her with his gaze and he must have looked ferocious because he could see her eyes go wide. "But I don't need a DNA test on this, Ramona. Because it's only been you. The whole time. Since that first night in Mountain Mama Pizza, in case you forgot."

"You know perfectly well I haven't forgotten."

"And what I'd like to know," Knox said as if she hadn't spoken, moving closer to her, "is how you can be the same person who told me you were in love with me when all along you thought *this* little of me."

She made a soft sound, like he'd delivered a gut punch.

But he didn't stop. "You really think that I'm the kind of man who had something going on with you that was as intense as it always was with us and was also running around banging nameless girls in bars who I couldn't identify in a lineup?" He shook his head. "That's who you think I am. That's the kind of love you have to give."

She flinched as if he'd hit her, and he didn't like that very much. But this was Ramona, so she didn't fall apart. She leaned closer, folded her arms over her chest, and blasted him right back.

"And why wouldn't I think that?" she demanded. "Who do you imagine made sure that I thought *exactly* that? You went out of your way to make me think the worst of you, Knox. You can't blame me now that I do."

Knox shook his head, his gaze intent on hers. "I don't know why Shoshana Delaney, whoever the hell she is, put me down as the father of this child. And it doesn't look like there's a whole lot I'm going to be able to do about that tonight, in case you didn't notice the whole blizzard outside while you drove over here. I don't even know if I'll be able to go look at any records before New Year's. So it looks like, like it or not, I get to play daddy for the foreseeable future. Because for some reason, this girl picked me."

He moved closer to Ramona, because he couldn't help himself. Because he could never help himself.

"I called you because I needed your help," he told her, and could hear his voice going lower. "I'm fully aware that you don't want anything to do with me, and I deserve that. But I don't think I deserve you believing that I would lie about something like this. Or anything else. I'm a lot of things and I certainly didn't treat you as well as you should be treated, but I never *lied* to you, Ramona."

"Technically, no," she agreed, her voice quieter, and yet somehow it seemed to pierce him right through. "Technically, you never did."

Technically was doing a lot of work, Knox thought.

"You don't have to help me," he told her then. "I didn't drag you out of bed to relitigate our shit. I'm sure my brothers can help me out once the sun comes up again. If it does." He tried to do something neutral with his face but wasn't sure he got there. "I appreciate you coming at all. I was worried something was wrong with her."

"I'm delighted to be of service." Ramona did not sound even remotely delighted.

They were standing very close together now, and he

knew the exact moment she realized how dangerous that was. Because it always was. He watched her cheeks flush and then she looked away, and without even meaning to he tracked the way her pulse beat in her neck.

Too fast. Too hot. He knew that because he liked to put his mouth there while he—

But no good could come of finishing that thought.

She stepped back and looked around as if she'd forgotten where she was. Then she headed toward the front door.

"Where are you going?" he asked quietly.

"Home," she said, without turning around.

"Not tonight, you're not." He didn't say that like it was a question, because it wasn't. "You probably shouldn't have come up here, though I'm glad you did. Can't you hear the wind? I don't think the storm has calmed down any."

Ramona still had her arms folded over her chest. She looked back at him with a dubious expression on her face and he wasn't the least bit surprised when she kept walking toward the front door, but instead of throwing it open to look out at the porch—or run for it—she peered out the window instead.

Knox saw the way she sighed more than he heard it. It was the way her shoulders drooped, and every single part of him wanted to go to her, but he didn't.

Not only because there was a tiny baby on his couch, sleeping with her chubby arms thrown up over her head, her face serious in slumber.

Hailey, he thought. *Her name is Hailey.*

He found himself rubbing the heel of his hand into the shallow valley between his pecs, and he wasn't sure why he felt *caught* when Ramona turned back around to see him doing it.

"Two-month-olds eat at regular intervals," she said, back to doctor mode. He didn't blame her. "Why don't we camp out here in the living room? I'll set up a diaper changing station, and show you how to make a bottle."

"I'd appreciate that," he said.

So formal.

But they both stood there for what seemed like too long, and he could feel that same pull toward her that he always did. He figured she felt it too, and neither one of them seemed to be all that happy about it.

So Knox broke the spell.

He made himself step back, step away, and then discovered that it was also hard to walk away from little Hailey, so he was pretty much screwed on all sides.

"I'll pull some bedding out here," he made himself say, and then he walked back into the dark recesses of his house.

Where he found himself grateful for the opportunity to take a deep breath at last.

But that didn't last. Because when he did, it was all Ramona.

Chapter Four

RAMONA KNEW THAT they'd lost power again sometime near dawn when the wind outside started howling again, and then she heard the generator begin to roar.

Knox had made them a vast pallet on the floor in front of the fire, and it was far more comfortable than it should have been. He'd built a kind of playpen/crib for little Hailey in the middle, and without discussing it, he and Ramona had slept on either side.

Though it had been fitful sleeping at best.

This time when she woke, she saw Knox was already up, and a quick glance indicated that he had already figured out the diaper situation. That put him head and shoulders above some of the new fathers she encountered, though she had to lecture herself not to make that something it wasn't. It was the bare minimum after all.

Ramona had gone to sleep cranky beyond measure, and confused, and filled with the wild gamut of emotions she always felt when in Knox's presence, but it seemed like what amounted to only a few catnaps in between feedings had given her some clarity.

She believed him.

Maybe that was naïve. Or maybe it was a form of wishful thinking. But she didn't think so.

Because one thing about Knox was that he had always been brutally clear on the fact that either one of them could see whoever else they wanted to, whenever they wanted to. That he didn't do permanent, didn't see that changing, and couldn't make any promises.

She was forced to agree with the notion that if he'd been sleeping with other women in that time, he wouldn't lie about it now.

The proof of that was also in the way he was singing to little Hailey as he changed her, as if he had nothing better to do in the whole world but cater to this little baby who had been literally abandoned and left at his door. He'd tossed himself into this without any hesitation. That didn't strike her as the kind of man who would shirk his duty. *Especially* not if he had any reason at all to believe that the baby might be his.

She didn't move from where she was curled up in a ball, a deliciously cozy throw blanket draped over her, because she wasn't ready to face him. Not just yet.

Because it was one thing to believe him, but a whole other thing to think about what that *meant*.

He had said that he hadn't slept with anyone else in the time they'd been doing their on-and-off thing, so the whole of the past year and a half. Neither had she, of course.

And she should have known better by now than to do

this. To make things that he said into whole declarations when he'd simply been stating facts. She knew by now that he never meant things the way she wished he did.

But still. She took that information away and held it close, because it made her feel good. Because it made her heart beat a little bit harder and a whole lot sweeter.

She wasn't breaking her stretch of Knox Carey sobriety if she acknowledged that it felt good to hear that from him. This was already the first interaction they'd ever had without a sexual component. She thought she was doing great.

Ramona sat up and stretched, and then turned around to find Knox standing over in the kitchen part of the great room with its high, pitched ceiling and grand windows, watching her with that brooding look on his face.

"Merry Christmas," she said. He frowned at that, so she pressed on to more pressing matters. "I don't suppose the weather's cleared up?"

Meaning, could she go home now? She ignored the little pang inside when she thought about leaving.

"The winds have died down in the past hour or so," he told her. "But the snow keeps on coming." She tried to keep her face impassive, but she obviously failed, because his mouth curved. "It's supposed to turn to freezing rain for a while and then temperatures are supposed to plummet this afternoon."

She knew what that meant. The snow might stop, but the freezing rain was treacherous, and when the temperature dropped it would all turn to ice. Making those roads she'd barely made it over last night into death traps.

Like it or not, she was stuck here.

Something she'd known was possible when she'd driven out here, but that didn't make her any happier about it now.

Ramona took a breath, then nodded. "Looks like you have that diaper change down already," she said, putting the focus on the baby, where it belonged. "You picked that up fast."

"Harlan said that no one was allowed in his house after Kiel was born unless they knew how to change a diaper," Knox said, his eyes gleaming. "Turned out, I'm the only one who needed teaching. Everyone else changed mine."

Ramona shook her head. "I'm sure they all brought that up as often as possible."

"Nonstop," he replied.

It wasn't until they both laughed that Ramona remembered herself. She looked away, clearing her throat. "I'm going to go clean up," she said. "Then, if you don't mind, I might see if I can rustle up some breakfast. I'm starving."

"Sounds like a plan," was all Knox said.

And it was an odd little Christmas, and not what she'd expected—but in some ways, Ramona thought it was one of the sweetest she'd ever had.

Knox talked to his brothers and his parents. Rosie had given birth to the new set of Carey twins—girls, this time— and they were all safe and sound down in the hospital in

Marietta. The rest of the Careys agreed to hunker down where they were instead of getting together the way Ramona thought they all clearly wanted to. There was a lot of talk of potentially snowshoeing up to the ranch house, but Belinda herself finally called it.

"Our Christmas celebration will have to be postponed," she announced. Ramona could hear her voice clearly through the phone that Knox had carried into his office. "It doesn't make sense to have it without Ryder and Rosie and the new babies anyway."

It was clear that all the brothers thought this was a good plan.

Knox didn't circle any of his family in on what was happening with little Hailey. Ramona didn't blame him for that. What was there to say without more information? And why blow it all up on Christmas when no one could do anything about it anyway?

Besides, for all they knew, the mysterious Shoshana Delaney would come back.

She cooked breakfast, then called her parents and checked in with their quiet festivities back in New Hampshire. Later, Knox made lunch. They traded turns with the baby without discussing it. They made notes about her sleep and feeding habits in the little notebook Ramona put on the coffee table after Knox produced it from his office.

When evening fell again outside, dark and bitter cold and early, they made dinner, too. It turned into something of a feast. He grilled a few steaks and some vegetables out on the grill that he had to shovel a path to. She threw together ingredients that she found in his cupboards and freezer to make a simple crumble.

He poured them both a little bit of spiced rum—more a tasting sample than a drink, clearly a nod to the infant that was the reason they were together right now, because they had certainly let alcohol lead them down all kinds of paths before—and they sat and ate before the fire with the baby gurgling in between them and playing with her toes.

Ramona had planned to spend Christmas the way she had last year. Tucked up in her cozy upstairs space in her grandfather's old house that she'd painstakingly renovated herself, eating the delicacies she'd picked up down in Marietta earlier in the week, and watching holiday movies on repeat. Or catching up on podcasts, like her current favorite—a local one on true crime that the Cowboy Point deputy sheriff's sister, Esther, had been hosting for a few years now. Or losing herself in the stack of brightly colored novels that she'd bought from Rosie's book shop—some from her pop-up Airstream at the Farm & Craft Market in the summer and some from her new location in one of the Lodge's cottages this fall, before she'd had to do some bed rest ahead of the new twins' arrival.

Ramona spent so much time with so many people thanks to her job that she found solitude to be an extravagant indulgence. She'd been looking forward to it.

But the truth was, this was better.

And if she let herself, Ramona was sure that she could have fallen head over heels into this little scene of domestic bliss without even noticing it was happening. Not until it was too late.

She had to keep a hard, painful grip on herself to keep from plummeting off that cliff, because she already knew that the landing sucked.

Because this was pretty much the exact dream she'd had about Knox since day one. This cozy togetherness that didn't require words or activities and, yes, a baby or two to make them a family. She'd seen wedding bells at first glance.

There'd been times she'd felt a lot of shame about those feelings, but she couldn't beat herself up about that now. Because no matter what he said when she tried to talk to him about these things, they worked.

She could feel how well they worked even now, on precious little sleep and too much careful sidestepping of their history. No matter what else happened, the ease she felt in his presence never ebbed.

Sure, he was beautiful in that way that should have felt dangerous and untrustworthy, but he'd never felt that way to her. Even if she didn't exactly love his harsh honesty—he would call it simply *honesty*—and had tried her best to hate him, she'd never quite gotten there.

And she really had tried.

Deep down, she'd always imagined that the two of them

could be happy together if they gave it a real chance. This unexpected Christmas wasn't doing her any favors in that department.

It would have been better if it was all a little less blissful.

But she couldn't bring herself to break the spell.

Hailey started fussing, and Ramona watched as Knox settled her down, soothing her to sleep on his wide shoulder.

"My mother is already determined to redo Christmas," he said, his gaze on the fire. Ramona could have told him she'd overheard that, but it seemed... too intimate, somehow. "She never misses a chance for a holiday. And I can't blame her. Not when my dad..." He shook his head.

Cowboy Point was a small town. Ramona knew that Zeke Carey had supposedly been given a year to live, and had hit that year mark last Easter. She also knew that he looked remarkably healthy for someone who was on that particular journey.

But he wasn't her patient. And no one had directly asked for her opinion, so she kept it to herself.

"Families are important," she said instead.

He looked at her then, over Hailey's little tuft of coppery hair. "You don't talk that much about yours." His mouth curved into something self-deprecating. "Or you don't talk to me about your family, anyway."

"I thought everybody knew," Ramona said. When Knox just continued looking at her in that way, as if he was drinking her in—a look that had gotten her in trouble more times than she could count—she blew out a breath. "My mom grew up here. The way she tells it, she couldn't wait to get out of this no-stoplight, no-stop-sign little town. She left when she was eighteen, moved to Boston for college, and never looked back. She met my dad there. They had me, and we stayed in Boston until I was six. Then we moved up to New Hampshire, where my father is a professor and my mother works in development at a private school in the area. Neither one of them has ever come back to Cowboy Point. I'm not sure my father has ever set foot in Montana, to be honest."

"How did you end up liking it so much if your mom hated it?" Knox asked.

"I'm sure I told you before that I spent my summers out here with my grandfather," Ramona said, frowning at him. Because it wasn't like they hadn't talked over the past year and a half. Not that she knew if he'd retained any of that.

But he nodded. "You did."

He shifted the baby, who made a few soft, gurgling sounds but didn't wake up as he transferred her back into that little crib of pillows between them. Then that intense hazel gaze of his consumed her from his side of the barrier. "I guess I'm just surprised that she would let you come back here when she went to so much trouble to stay away herself."

"She's often said that she never would have let me come back here in the summers if she thought I'd end up moving here," Ramona replied with a laugh. "And I don't know that

I blame her for how she feels about this place."

She thought of Cat, who Ramona had first met when the other girl was at something of a crossroads in her life. Cat had laid out how hard it was to be a local, known by everybody, and yet *truly* known by few. Held securely in place by her family name, and all that history, and yet held back from any dreams she might have had by those same names and histories.

"Some people like living in a place where everyone knows their story," Ramona said. "But not everybody does. I get that."

He was studying her and she could feel it like a touch. She had to remind herself that it wasn't. "Do you normally go back home for Christmas?" he asked.

"I haven't in a long time." She was sitting cross-legged on the floor in the same long johns and T-shirt she'd been wearing since she arrived and had shrugged out of the merino wool sweater she usually wore as a base layer. There was no particular reason she should feel so overheated, suddenly, but Knox was giving her all of his attention. She'd always been susceptible to that. "For a long time I was on call at Christmas. It was easier not to set any expectations, so I'd usually go and see my parents at other times. When it's easier to get in and out of airports, and drive into the New Hampshire wilderness, such as it is."

He didn't look overheated as he leaned back against the couch and stuck his legs out toward the fire. He looked lazy and intrigued. "How does it stack up?"

"Don't get me wrong," she said, and laughed. "I wouldn't want to get stranded in some of New Hampshire's less settled places. A mountain is a mountain, even in the east. But nothing is as *formidable* as Montana." She studied him. "You want to travel more, don't you?"

The windows rattled, indicating the wind was gusting, and he seemed to take his time looking at her again. "It's a big world. Folks around here think that a big sky is all they need, but I've always thought it was impossible to make that determination unless you did both."

"Can the ranch make it without you?" She didn't know if she was kidding when she said that or not, but she was surprised when Knox laughed.

He stretched back out on his side of the blankets, forgoing the couch as a back support entirely, and stacked his hands beneath his head.

"If you asked my brothers, they'd tell you that I don't work here on the ranch now," he said. "So no, I don't think they'd miss my contributions."

Ramona had heard him say things like that before. She'd heard his brothers say things like that too, for that matter. And it occurred to her that this was the first time they'd really had an extended conversation like this without there being nudity involved.

Her sobriety initiative where he was concerned was going well, Ramona thought a bit smugly. This was the equivalent of being able to sit at a dinner where wine was served without having to turn her glass upside down to keep from taking a sip.

Because when there was nudity involved, they never talked very long.

Because there were always better things to do.

And there had always, always been nudity involved until now.

But then, for the first time, it occurred to her that maybe that had been part of the problem.

They had spent a lot of time together, but when she looked back, it seemed to her that there was a whole lot of shallow water when they were together and then deep feelings in between.

On her part anyway.

"Do you think that your brothers are misrepresenting your contributions, then?" she asked, hoping that he couldn't see what she was thinking about all over her face.

He laughed again. "Of course I do."

But he didn't elaborate.

And normally, Ramona would have let that go. Talked of something else or, more likely, kissed him instead.

It didn't escape her that she might actually have found her own culpability here. Hurting her own feelings for over a year and not realizing the extent of it until now.

But everything was different today, thanks to little Hailey. So that meant she could be different too. "I think sometimes that families can get into a rut," she said after a moment. "I can hear the way I talk about my mom. I make it sound like she's filled with hate and is constantly railing against all things Montana." She wrinkled up her nose. "That's not really true. She's the first person I want to call when something happens. I like to make her laugh and she always makes me laugh. That was a lifeline during my residency. And she can make anything grow. She brings plants back to life when I swear they've turned to ash and dirt. She sings to them, which she claims is the secret. I, on the other hand, have a black thumb and kill plants with impunity." She considered that, too aware of the heat of his gaze on her. "My mother and I are both uncomfortably alike and completely different. I imagine all families are like that."

"I love my brothers," Knox said, very matter-of-factly. He shifted so he could look at Ramona directly. "I know they love me too, despite what you might be led to believe if you listen to them talk shit. But you, to them, I'm the one who *had* to do things differently. Who *had* to go off to college. Who *needed* to create a source of income that has nothing to do with the ranch."

"Your brother Ryder was a huge rodeo star," Ramona reminded him. "I feel certain he had another source of income as a bull rider at that level. Your brother Boone opened his own dairy. You're not the only one that's gone out on his own."

"But the things I do don't benefit the ranch, to their way

of thinking," Knox said, and it was the fact that he didn't even sound resigned that got to her. He sounded... matter-of-fact. Understanding, even. "It raises High Mountain Ranch's profile to have a rodeo star around the place. Same thing with Boone's dairy and all the rest of the things he and Sierra are trying to do. Me, on the other hand?" He gave a sort of philosophical shrug that made her heart ache. "The reality is that any work that you don't have to do with your own two hands is a little suspect in the Carey family."

Ramona couldn't contain her frown. "That's just stupid."

And this time when Knox laughed, it was a different sort of laugh altogether. This one was pure delight, as if she had surprised him.

"I said I loved my brothers," he replied. "I didn't say they weren't idiots."

And Ramona thought that it was a good thing that they'd both only had the faintest, slightest taste of that rum, because otherwise, she wasn't sure she wouldn't have backslid entirely.

She was grateful when Hailey woke up mad, demanding a diaper change and a cuddle.

There was more snow the next day, piling up higher and higher outside. The power came back on in fits and starts, only to get knocked out again when the wind picked up or the freezing rain swept in, turning the trees into sculptures that gleamed.

Time became meaningless.

They revolved around Hailey's schedule and slept when they could. Ramona had often wondered how new parents did it—now she was getting a crash course.

But she found it all a kind of wonder. To be this close to such a new human that she started to understand the difference in the sounds she made. To understand how to communicate, broadly and roughly, with a creature who couldn't speak or understand words.

She wasn't sure she'd ever loved a brand-new human more.

By the time the storm finally cleared, the snow stopped, and the temperature rose up high enough to melt the worst of the dangerous ice and leave the snow reasonably passable, it was December 28th.

She'd been living with Knox for days. Knox and a small baby, like a fever dream of domestic bliss.

Ramona's personal tragedy was that it was far too easy.

Even though she tried her best to caution herself against thinking such things, she couldn't help but note that they made a great team. They took care of the baby, made food and cleaned up after themselves, tagging in and out seamlessly.

She told herself it wasn't real life. If Hailey was really their baby, it would be different. Both of them were, on some level, viewing this as a temp position. And everybody knew that temps were only good at their jobs until they assumed a permanent position, at which point they hated it as much as everybody else.

She tried to tell herself that was the only thing going on here, but she smelled like him now because she'd used his soap and his shampoo. *Temping* didn't ring true.

Her body was settled in like this was her new home now. Her new life.

But the morning of the 28th was clear. And warmer than it had been for days.

Ramona knew it was time she went home.

"I've gotten a little bit attached to you," she told Hailey, as the little girl blew bubbles up at her and kicked her feet. "I think you're going to have to put up with me going forward, no matter where you're living."

Though she didn't like thinking that it wouldn't be here.

Knox had pulled on his boots and a heavy sweater before he'd headed outside. A glance out the window showed her that he was digging her truck out.

Ramona was beginning to think that claims to sobriety concerning him were a little bit silly. Sure, she hadn't imbibed. But she was basically floating in a barrel of all things Knox, letting him sink into her pores.

It was past time to go.

He came back inside, and there was a look on his face that she couldn't have described if her life depended on it, but she could *feel* it. She could feel *him*.

She tucked Hailey into her makeshift crib and kissed her.

Once, then again.

And if she felt like crying when she stood again, she blinked it away. Then set about pulling on her outer layers while pretending Knox wasn't *right there*.

Taking up all the air in the room.

"Don't forget your backpack," he said.

"Oh." That was not what she meant to say, but he was closer than she thought when she straightened from pulling on her boots. "I'm leaving that here. You can bring the backpack to the clinic sometime, when you've used everything."

"That's very kind."

He did not look like he was thinking about *kindness*.

Ramona knew she wasn't.

She tugged on her various layers, shoved her hat on, wrapped her scarf around her neck, and was something like *relieved* to zip up her heavy coat. To be wearing an entire cold weather fortress.

Surely that would keep her safe from her own worst impulses.

Knox grabbed her medical bag and walked her out. Her truck was running, meaning he'd started it so it would be warm when she got in. He'd shoveled a path down from his porch and walked in front of her to swing her bag into the passenger seat.

Then he stood there as she came toward him, and she couldn't quite bring herself to round the hood.

"I'm glad you called me," she said.

"I am too."

She couldn't have looked away from him on pain of death. It was like she'd fallen into some kind of tractor beam. The urge to close the distance between them was so overwhelming that she wasn't sure she was strong enough to resist it.

But she did.

"I'm going to have to follow up with that baby," she said, stepping back. Getting her professional smile in place. "I think I'm a little bit in love."

That was the wrong thing to say to this man.

"I know," he said quietly, and she got the distinct impression that they weren't talking about the baby. There was something like anguish in his gaze. "But it doesn't change anything."

She wanted to fight him on that, but that was the old version of her. The not-at-all clean or sober version. The still-too-drunk-on-Knox-Carey version.

This Ramona only held his gaze a moment, then turned and made her way around to the driver's side. He didn't stop her. He didn't say a word.

No reason at all for her whole chest to hurt.

When she looked in the rearview mirror as she bumped her way across the snow toward the ranch's main drive, he was still there.

But she waited until she was back home, finally tucked

up in her cozy apartment above the clinic, to let herself go.

And allow herself to cry for what could never be until she had no tears left.

Chapter Five

KNOX STOOD OUTSIDE longer than he should have, watching her go. Then he found himself a little too cold when he jogged back inside, moving immediately to check on the baby once he shut the door behind him.

It occurred to him then that he hadn't been alone with Hailey since Christmas Eve. Since he found her on the doorstep and had spent those couple of hours trying to keep her calm before Ramona arrived.

He found himself smiling at the little girl, getting down close so he could put his hand on her cute, round little belly wrapped up in one of the little onesie pajamas that Ramona had brought with her, since it seemed the woman thought of everything.

And he felt like there was too much pressing in on him. He felt like Ramona was a ghost here now in this house he'd built himself and should not have had any kind of hauntings at all. He kept expecting to look up and find her still here, in the kitchen, or coming to settle down in this little baby area he'd made in front of the fire, when he knew perfectly well she was driving home.

The weather had finally cleared and that meant that it

was time to get back to reality. A reality that was markedly different than it had been a few days ago, at least for him.

Because whatever happened, one thing Knox knew was that he wasn't walking away from this child. Whoever had left her on his doorstep had signed up for his involvement in this child's life, forever.

He'd never really been someone to do anything by half.

His phone buzzed, and even though he knew with near certainty that it wouldn't be Ramona, he was still disappointed when it was the family text instead.

Ryder and Rosie and the babies are at the ranch house, Wilder texted. *Full family assembly required.*

That was when Knox realized that he was actually going to have to explain all this to his family. Or more accurately, it was when he realized that he had kind of been hoping to somehow avoid it.

But that wasn't reality.

And if the past few days had taught him anything, it was that asking for help was the right move. Even from his own family, though he could acknowledge that he hadn't really done that too often in the past.

It was part of being the youngest. He was offered so much unsolicited advice that it never occurred to him to ask for it when he actually wanted some. He'd informed his family that he was going to college when he received a scholarship, not before. There had been accusations of secrecy, but he'd never seen it that way. He'd never been hiding anything. It was just with so many strong opinions, he sometimes preferred his own.

But he wasn't sure baby Hailey qualified. He'd watched the way the family behaved around little Kiel this fall. Everyone pitched in. Everyone helped where they could. The kid was growing up with a village whether he liked it or not.

It was going to be the same with Ryder and Rosie's new twin girls.

And it wasn't that Knox had determined that he was going to become this child's father—since he knew he wasn't, in fact, her father—but that didn't mean Hailey shouldn't benefit from that kind of Carey consideration and care until he figured out what would become of her. She'd been left here all alone. That didn't mean she had to live here the same way.

After a quick internet search, Knox realized that he didn't have the appropriate equipment, so he was going to have to do his best with what he did have. He bundled them both up, then carried her outside, and rigged up a workable car seat situation on the passenger side of his truck. Maybe not optimal for any kind of distance, but he figured it would work to get him up to the ranch house.

Then he found himself following the tracks that Ramona had laid down along his drive to hook up with the main road that led up to the ranch house. Instead of following her down toward the little valley that made up Cowboy Point, he turned right and followed the grooves that were already carved out in the snow, no doubt Ryder driving his expanded family back from the Marietta hospital now that the weather had cleared.

When he got up to the ranch house, he could see smoke coming from the chimney and all the Christmas lights twinkling out into the bright morning the way they would for weeks yet, because Belinda liked her Christmas lights to stay up as long as possible. She usually started on Thanksgiving and ended sometime before Valentine's Day, depending on the year. He found a parking space next to all the other trucks, and braced himself a little, because it was a full house. He unstrapped Hailey, and smiled down at her as she made her little noises, wiggling around in her car seat.

"You're going to meet my family," he told her, in the solemn way he'd taken to talking to her. Like she understood him. "They're a lot. But don't worry. Underneath, they're solid."

She babbled something, then looked at him very closely and contemplatively, as if considering what he'd said.

Knox had the strangest sensation, like he could probably stand here and fall into that adorable little gaze in her sweet little face forever.

He picked her up out of the car seat and held her in the crook of his arm, adjusting the adorable blue hat with a huge pom-pom that Ramona had brought with her, so she was bundled up tight. Blue mittens too, which had obviously been intended for a baby boy—but beggars couldn't be choosers. She was zipped up in the tiny parka that went with these items, that Ramona had claimed had been in one of the grab bags she'd put together for situations like his.

Are there a lot of situations like mine? he'd asked.

I always like to be prepared, was all she'd said in reply, and he hadn't been able to tell if she didn't want to answer him or couldn't because she had to keep things confidential as a doctor.

Either way, he decided then and there that he should personally make sure that there were always more of these emergency packs available for whoever might need them in the future. Because they had certainly helped him out this time.

But he was stalling. He knew he was stalling, and it wasn't like this was going to get any easier, initially. He was going to have to rip the Band-Aid off and there was no time like the present, because it was cold out here.

So he sucked it up and he trudged across the yard, making his way through the snow to the back door, following the boot tracks his brothers had left before him.

And he blew out a breath when he reached out to open that door, then walked inside.

He could hear the whole family immediately—all the usual sounds of the Carey family chaos. He could hear his little nephews shouting, sounding sugared up, which meant either that they really had gotten into the candy or they were just excited to see their parents and their new baby sisters.

He could hear the rumble of his brothers' voices and his sisters-in-laws' softer tones. And interspersed with all of that, his mother's typical dire warnings to anyone who ventured too close to her stove and the sound of his father's deep, gruff laughter.

Knox peeled off his coat as best he could and tossed it with the rest of the outerwear in the mudroom. He spent more time getting Hailey out of hers, so she was left in her pink fleece with her coppery hair standing on end.

And he couldn't really deal with the boot situation since he didn't want to put her down, so he just walked in.

Straight on into the kitchen, where most of his family was gathered around the big kitchen table. Everything was bright, cheery, and boisterous.

Knox just waited.

Because one by one, they all turned to look at him. And grew quiet.

Really, he thought, this was pretty funny. He wished he had an extra hand to whip out his phone and take a picture when the quiet finally reached everyone, and every single member of his family was finally silent—a miracle in itself—and staring at him.

With a whole lot of open mouths, too.

He hadn't seen that before.

"Yes," he drawled into the shocked silence. "I am holding a baby. No, she's not mine. She was a Christmas present left on my doorstep on Christmas Eve." He could have sworn that even more mouths opened then and jaws dropped lower. "I mean that literally."

Hailey, apparently sensing a captive audience, blew a cute little bubble, then giggled.

And then everything kind of exploded. Too many voices. A great many exclamations. A wild din of demands for clarification and some comments he was glad he couldn't quite hear.

It wasn't until Belinda detached herself from the rest of them, stepping away from her beloved stove and marching over to him, that it quieted down a little bit.

"Let me see that baby," Belinda demanded.

She didn't wait for Knox to hand the baby over. She plucked Hailey into her arms and beamed down at her. And like every other being who encountered Belinda Carey, Hailey blinked, then beamed back.

"My goodness," Belinda cooed. "What a sweet little love you are!"

There were other, smaller babies in the room that he had yet to meet, so Knox left Hailey with his mom. He ignored all of the suspicious looks being thrown his way so he could go over to the kitchen table. Rosie was sitting there with one adorable bundle of a red-faced, scrunchy-looking baby in her arms, while next to her, Ryder held the other.

"Look at these perfect little beings you made," Knox said softly, and Rosie beamed. Ryder, he noticed, just gazed at Knox coolly over his babies' heads.

"Their names are Holly and Ivy, because Christmas got the better of us and we couldn't resist," Rosie said, sounding besotted. "And so far they are perfect little angels, unlike their brothers. Or maybe we just got more sleep in the hospital this time around."

And Knox didn't much like the look on Ryder's face, so he nodded as he gazed down at the two little burrito-shaped babies.

"Must feel like a vacation not to have to do it all alone this time," he drawled.

Ryder gave him the finger. Rosie laughed. Knox stepped back, feeling pretty satisfied with himself, and then there was no avoiding the rest of his family, who had clearly only given him space to greet the newest arrivals.

"What do you mean she's not yours?" Boone asked in a low voice. Immediately. With that *disappointed* look he liked to aim at Knox when he felt like Knox wasn't *stepping up*. Knox loved his brother. He also, in this moment, deeply felt the need to deck him. "Why would someone leave a baby on your doorstep if she wasn't yours?"

"Why are you saying that like leaving babies on doorsteps is a normal thing to do?" his wife, Sierra, interjected.

"Where there's smoke there's fire," Wilder drawled from where he was leaning against the wall that divided the kitchen and the living room, a bottle of beer in his hand and Cat at his side. *She* had a speculative look on her face, but was keeping her comments to herself. Knox had always liked

Cat. Wilder kept going. "And I'm not sure there's a bigger bonfire than driving all the way onto the ranch in inclement weather to leave a baby on a doorstep."

Knox hadn't had a full-on rumble with his brothers in some time, but today was looking more and more likely to break that drought.

Harlan was holding baby Kiel with his other arm around Kendall, and he only shook his head at Knox. Clearly the brotherly conclusion had been reached. They'd tried him and found him guilty without even asking.

That was what really tipped it over for him.

"I told you that she isn't mine," Knox said, very calmly. Very matter-of-factly. Very much like Dr. Ramona Taylor, in fact, but it did him no good to think about her just now. "I didn't say that for fun or because I'm in denial. There's no possible way that I'm the father of this baby. My name is on her birth certificate and someone figured they needed to put her in my possession, and I assume there's a reason for that. But that reason isn't because we share a scrap of DNA."

The ring of brothers and sisters-in-law around him went quiet. There was only the sound of Zeke talking to the two toddlers as they negotiated for treats by the fridge, and Belinda murmuring little songs to Hailey.

"Well," Wilder said, sounding a lot like he was trying to be as close to diplomatic as he ever got, "I suppose there's always a paternity test to know for sure."

Knox leveled a gaze on him. "I don't need a paternity

test," he said, sounding cooler and more precise with each word. "When I tell you I know exactly where I've been, I mean that. I'm going to need all of you to trust me on this. Because I'm not actually a twelve-year-old kid, in case you haven't noticed. I'm a grown-ass man who knows where I put my dick."

And normally, Belinda would object to such language during a family gathering and mete out her usual brand of swift justice—but a look from the corner of his eye told Knox that his mother was hiding a grin.

But then, Knox wasn't being loud. He hadn't started shouting. The only thing he was doing was talking to his brothers in a manner that was a big sea change from the usual charm offensive he pulled out in uncomfortable family moments. Or the way he usually laughed it off when they said things to him he didn't love.

Because this wasn't about him.

"If she was my daughter, I would have no problem claiming her," he informed them all. "As it is, she's my responsibility since she was left at my house and my name is connected to hers on that birth certificate. I'd like to get to the bottom of that mystery, but while I do, I'll be taking care of her. Just like I've been taking care of her for the past few days."

And it felt to him like something shifted. He could feel it all around. Even from Ryder over the table with his newborns.

Knox moved away from the knot of brothers to go and give his father a hug. Zeke pounded him on the back, and clapped his shoulder for good measure. "I'm proud of you," his father said. "It's not always easy to do the right thing, but it's never the wrong choice."

He hadn't needed that validation, but he sure liked getting it.

Ryder and Rosie didn't stay long. Ryder carefully transported the new babies and Rosie out to his truck, then came back in to prevail upon his sons to be good men for a little while longer as he and their mama got settled.

The twins looked at each other with identical looks of mischief, clearly perfectly happy to stay put.

Ryder also came over and shook Knox's hand.

"You wouldn't believe how much baby stuff we have," Ryder told him. "I swear we've got quadruples of most things. I'll put them on the porch so you can come grab what you need. Help set you up right." He inclined his head. "Until you get to the bottom of it all."

"Same," Harlan chimed in, nodding at Knox. "We'd love to help outfit you."

"Appreciate it," Knox replied.

Which was about as heartfelt an apology as his brothers had in them, but Knox was more than good with it.

Despite the expected rocky start, he felt surprised to discover just how clear it was that he'd done the right thing by coming up here this morning. By not trying to hide Hailey from anyone. By involving his entire family in this wild thing that was happening to him.

Because as they all sat around the kitchen table as the morning moved along into afternoon, Hailey was fussed over by everybody. There was no shortage of arms to hold her or delighted family members to take their turn coaxing smiles from her, or giving her a bottle, or even changing her diaper.

Knox found that he tracked her without even thinking about it. He knew where she was at all times, and could pick out her cry from Kiel's without a problem.

His mother found him on the living room couch at one point. He was holding Hailey, who'd needed a little break from the excitement to finally fall into an exhausted sleep. Belinda sat down next to him, bumping her shoulder against his.

He had the sudden memory then of being a small boy, not much older than his nephews, and his mother sitting down with him just like this—bumping their shoulders together then, too. Though way back then she'd been the bigger one. Now he dwarfed her.

It felt like such an interesting inversion. Such a funny little slip in time and space, particularly with the little baby under his care in his arms.

"How on earth did you manage with this sweet little thing for the past few days without any help?" Belinda asked. "I would have taken a sled down the hill to help you out, Knox. You must know that."

"I do know that," Knox assured her. "But you didn't need to be out gallivanting around in all that bad weather."

Belinda made an offended noise, because she knew as well as he did that what he was really saying was that he didn't want his mother risking herself in her advanced years—something he would never actually *say* to her, as she was only in her mid-sixties.

"Besides," he said, going back to the neutral voice that had worked so well before. "I called Dr. Taylor. She came and helped out."

Belinda's hazel eyes gleamed. She gazed at him for a moment that started toward uncomfortable—her specialty—then dropped it to the baby. Hailey was at maximum cuteness, passed out like a drunk with her mouth open and letting out the sweetest little snores Knox had ever heard.

"Isn't it interesting," Belinda mused. When Knox only looked at her, unwilling to give an inch when they both knew she was digging, his mother smiled. "Who you think to call in a crisis," she clarified. "It really cuts through all the noise, doesn't it? Because you find out who really matters."

Before Knox could answer her, she was on her feet, racing off to swat Zeke's hands away from the dessert tray he'd already visited about ten times.

Meaning Knox couldn't do anything but sit there and marinate in what she'd said. Whether he liked it or not.

It was a truth he hadn't seen coming and didn't quite know what to do with.

When people started to trickle out, Belinda commandeered Hailey, and waved him away.

"I'm sure you have things to do," she said. "You didn't expect a baby and can't possibly have been prepared for one. Meanwhile, I could start preschool in this house. Right this very moment, if I wanted to. That's how prepared I am for grandchildren. Leave her with me. Come back and get her later. Miss Hailey and I are going to get acquainted."

That hadn't really been Knox's plan. And he found there was something inside of him that didn't much like the idea, either. Not that he didn't trust his mother, but he hadn't been separated from Hailey since she'd been left on his porch. It didn't sit well with him.

But he did have things to do. And he could definitely use some things for her in his house. She couldn't have a pillow crib on the living room floor forever.

He kissed his mother on the cheek and kept his reservations to himself, mostly because he was kind of surprised by them. "There are a few things I could probably see to," he agreed. "I think my first stop is going to be to see the deputy sheriff, to see if he's ever heard of Shoshana Delaney."

Because if Atticus Wayne hadn't heard of someone in Cowboy Point or out in the mountains around here, they were either a tourist passing through or they didn't exist.

"Sounds like a plan," Boone boomed out from behind him, surprising him. When Knox looked over at him in surprise, Boone only nodded, looking as solid as a rock and a lot like one of the mountains around here, which had always been the vibe Boone Carey brought to any party he attended.

"If Atticus can't work his law enforcement magic," Wilder said from where he was lounging on the couch, "I'm sure we can head down into Marietta and see if Dawson O'Dell himself has any idea who she is. Maybe cast a wider net down there in the actual sheriff's office."

There was no dissuading them. Even when Knox tried, both of his older brothers piled into his truck and made it clear that there would be no dislodging them.

And as Knox drove down into Cowboy Point, all he could think was that this was the part that actually mattered.

His brothers like to talk shit. They did it all the time, and would no doubt continue doing it. Truth was, when it wasn't directed at him, Knox kind of loved it.

Because talking shit was a love language and the other side of that coin was this. His brothers offering their full support, showing him that they believed him with their bodies and their time. Making it clear that a Carey brother only walked alone if he wanted to.

If he hadn't thought they would mock him mercilessly for the rest of his earthly days, Knox might have shed a little tear at that.

He almost did anyway just to see if Boone would launch himself out of the truck in protest.

Down in town, they found Atticus Wayne in the official Cowboy Point Deputy Sheriff's Office, a small outpost that was tucked in beside the tiny regional library. Both served the community and the folks way out in the hills, though Knox figured most people were happier when they saw Sara Jane Stark, the librarian, coming than they were to catch sight of Atticus. Atticus was around Harlan's age and had been a fixture in Knox's life for as long as he could remember. He looked like what he was: ex-military, current law enforcement, and a Montana man straight through.

Knox had imagined that he would have to go through a whole new round of justifications and explanations as he insisted that he was not the father no matter what it said on Hailey's birth certificate, but it wasn't necessary.

Atticus started nodding the moment he said the name Shoshana Delaney.

"I know the Delaneys," he said in his gruff voice. "There's a whole pile of them that live out near Devil's Gorge. Not a happy place. Not a happy family. If Shoshana is who I think she is out of that crew, she's already had a tough time of it."

"I don't want to add to her tough time," Knox said after a moment, digesting what he knew about Devil's Gorge, places like it, and what that probably meant for the poor girl who'd been so desperate she'd given up her baby the way she had. "But I would like to know why she picked my name out of the hat."

Behind him, Boone made a noise. "Devil's Gorge isn't just off the grid. It's off the hook. Folks go out there sometimes and don't come back."

"That is unfortunately a fact," Atticus agreed. He leveled a look at Knox. "I don't blame you for wanting answers. But I'm not sure you'll find any. The Delaneys aren't the friendliest or most welcoming bunch. I find it's best to talk to them from the right side of a jail cell and even then, they're not exactly forthcoming."

When Knox only shrugged, because there were presently no Delaneys in the tiny holding cell, Atticus pulled out a map. Then they all took some time debating how best to get out to a place where the inhabitants didn't want to be found and the geography was inhospitable enough to feel like collusion. All without driving off into oblivion in mountains that were particularly unfriendly right now, in these dead days of late December.

"If you must go out there," Atticus said, "and I can see that you're going to, watch your backs."

"A full-time occupation," Wilder assured him with a grin.

They all went back outside and took a few bracing sort of breaths in the frigid air. Right there by the library where Knox could look across the road and see the sign at the end of Ramona's drive, beckoning patients into her clinic.

He had to stand there and take a few breaths to clear his head of her, instead of preparing for whatever lay ahead in Devil's Gorge, a place most locals weren't foolish enough to go looking for.

Boone and Wilder stood with him, and he didn't know what they were thinking. He wasn't about to ask, either. They all watched as Matilda Stark drove by in her antique red pickup, her usual disheveled braids poking out from beneath a brightly colored knit hat, with what looked like an entire litter of dogs in the back seat. She saw them all standing there and waved through the window with that big, wide smile of hers that some folks found weird.

Knox had always found her adorable, though he'd been wise enough to keep that opinion to himself. She had far too many large and disreputable cousins, and they all liked to brawl.

The air was so cold that it hurt his face, but it also made him feel alive. *Awake.* He also felt like it made his brain work at its normal capacity for the first time in a few days.

And he wanted nothing more than to go across the road and tell Ramona where they were going and why.

Then he remembered, with a kind of thud in the center of his chest, what his mother had said about the person he wanted to call first. And for help and…maybe just in general.

You find out who really matters, Belinda had said.

It occurred to him then that maybe playacting having a baby with a woman he didn't actually have a baby with, but had a whole long and complicated history with instead, had messed him up some.

But Wilder slapped him on the back and he had to let

that go. Beside him, Boone nodded, like the starting gun had sounded.

Boone looked at Knox with challenge in his gaze, like this was the best adventure they'd had since they were little kids battling pretend monsters in the barn.

"Guess we're going off-roading, little brother," he drawled. "So we better get into those mountains before it gets dark."

Chapter Six

I T WAS GETTING late that night when Ramona heard the knock on her door.

She knew immediately who it was.

Who it had to be—and the knowledge that he was here, *right there* on the other side of her door, made her breath catch and her pulse kick into high gear. The way it always did.

Because the knock came on the private, outside entrance to the second floor of her house, not downstairs at the clinic entrance. And there was only one person she could think of in all of Cowboy Point who would show up there unannounced. Much less this late.

It seemed like it had been a lifetime since she'd left Knox's house early yesterday morning. It had felt like she was tearing off her skin to simply… sink back into her actual life. The life she'd worked so hard to make here.

The life she knew, deep down, she loved fiercely, even if it didn't feel that way while in the middle of her first Knox hangover in a couple of months.

She'd seen some patients. She'd updated her endless backlog of notes. She had woken up today to more of the same, and had decided that it was probably a good thing that Cat had taken a couple of weeks off for the holidays. Ramona knew somehow that her colleague and friend would have a whole lot to say about the Knox of it all.

Ramona had wanted to check in on little Hailey more than she'd wanted to breathe, but she'd held herself back. She'd decided that she would call Knox when she was truly—and only—interested in the welfare of the child.

She wasn't quite there yet.

And now she stared at the door off her little kitchen, frozen solid in her living room. She really shouldn't let him in. She knew better than that. She'd worked so hard to make herself immune to him, and the only reason she'd gone out there on Christmas Eve was Hailey. Him showing up on her doorstep couldn't possibly lead anywhere good...

But the knock came again, and it wasn't like he didn't know she was in here. He could see that all her lights were on.

Besides, the real truth was, Ramona didn't have the strength not to let him in. She didn't have it in her to turn him away. She didn't know what that made her, but she got up and walked over to the door, padding across the wood floors in her cozy socks and then pulling the door open.

Knox stood there, an intense look on his face, and he was alone. No sign of the baby, though Ramona didn't know if that was a good thing or a bad thing.

Or how she felt about it, for that matter.

Ramona didn't know how she felt about anything, only that her entire body was reacting to him the way it always did—with entirely too much enthusiasm, need and joy and *delight*—but she stepped back, wordlessly, and let him in anyway.

She'd been kidding herself to think she might ever have done anything else. It was one thing to avoid him around town. It was something else to pretend she didn't hear him knocking.

That was why she'd picked up his call on Christmas Eve, if she was being honest with herself.

Ramona didn't have it in her to regret that, either.

As always, Knox was so intensely male that it called the softness of this apartment she'd made into her retreat into high relief. He smelled like the dark and the snow, and the night seemed to rush in all around him before he could close the door behind him.

She watched as he shrugged out of his coat and hung it up on the pegs near the door. He kicked off his boots as well, then ran his hands through his messy dark hair after he took off his hat and the gaiter he wore around his neck to keep the weather out.

Knox looked around, the way he always did, like he found her apartment a surprise every time.

She kind of thought that what took him by surprise every time was the *girliness* of it all. Not exactly the hallmark of the very Western, very Montanan, very male ranch house he'd grown up in. Not to mention the modernized version of that he'd made himself.

Ramona thought it was probably all the *pink*.

This apartment had been her big project after she finished pulling the clinic together downstairs. She'd done it herself, over the course of about a year, and she was more than pleased with the result. She had started with all the old carpeting everywhere. Once she'd pulled it all up she'd found sunny wood floors beneath, and that had been her guide for the rest.

She'd made everything bright, with a rosy sort of glow to combat the gloom of the long winters. She'd painted the walls a pale pink that seemed to make its own sunshine when the world outside was dark and gloomy and cold. She'd refashioned the staircase outside, turning it from more of a fire escape into an actual covered stair so she could always have a separate entrance to her home. She'd thought it might be preferable if she ever had a patient stay overnight downstairs. Something that wasn't out of the question given how far away Marietta could seem in the dead of winter. She'd also maintained the interior staircase, though she'd put a door at the bottom so that she could go back and forth if she liked without having to brave the cold.

Inside, she'd made everything soft, cozy, and serene. Pale colors that complemented each other and felt like a long, deep exhale every time she came inside.

But Knox always made the apartment seem excessively

feminine. Almost frothy.

Neither one of them had spoken yet, she realized then.

They were just… *staring* at each other, and Ramona realized it was probably because this was already nothing like all the other times he'd shown up at her door. They were normally kissing by now, or he'd have hauled her up so she could wrap her legs around him, and they'd be staggering deeper into the apartment and maybe making it all the way to her bedroom. Or maybe not.

She cleared her throat and then motioned him toward the table there in her happy little kitchen, and when she found herself backing up like she didn't dare turn around, she made herself stop. Then she turned around and walked over to her counter, calmly, instead of racing around because there was too much adrenaline in her now that he was here.

"Do you want something warm to drink?" she asked, as if she had no greater concerns in all the world, nor ever would. As if she hardly noticed that her large, dangerously hot ex had turned up in her kitchen in the middle of the night, and not in possession of the baby who might have made this something other than a personal visit. "It looks hideously cold out there."

"It's cold," Knox agreed, and she thought he sounded a little raspier than usual. She ordered herself not to focus on that. "I wouldn't say no to coffee."

Ramona was already aware that this man could chug gallons of coffee all through the night, then immediately lie down and sleep like a baby. She had commented on it too many times already, so it seemed wiser not to say anything now.

He went and took a chair at the table, turning it backwards and straddling it. She busied herself at the counter, making him a real coffee and herself a decaf from her machine, and she could feel it press in all around her as she worked. That sense of intimacy that she always felt when the two of them were alone. Alone, clothed, and sharing the same air like this.

It was the kind of congenial quiet that gave a girl ideas, and she'd already had far too many of those ideas for her own good.

None of which had ever come to anything, lest she forget.

She brought the coffees over in two mugs and set them down on the sweet, tiled table that she'd bought from an artist at the Farm & Craft Market her first summer.

Then she sat down too. And waited, with the coziness of her kitchen all around her and the deep tragedy of Knox Careys extreme and offensive gorgeousness right there in front of her.

Ramona reminded herself that she still hadn't broken the vow she'd made to herself. She hadn't touched him since October and given the recent provocation and testing of those boundaries, she thought that required celebration.

Though maybe she needed to get through tonight first.

"Are you all right?" she asked him when he didn't speak, only gazed at her as if he was... looking for something. Better not to speculate what, she thought. "Did something happen to Hailey?"

"She's with my mom," Knox said. "I may have to fight her to get the baby back, in fact, but she's safe and sound. I just FaceTimed them from the truck." He took a pull from his coffee and then set it back down. "Wilder, Boone, and I tracked down the Delaneys."

Ramona wasn't expecting that. Her eyes widened. "Oh wow. Did you find Shoshana?"

Knox shook his head, his gaze on hers. "Do you know where Devil's Gorge is?"

When Ramona shook her head, he sighed. Then shifted a little in his chair. "It's a good three-hour drive west. Not because it's that far as the crow flies, but because there's no direct route. It's all fire access roads and suggestions of trails with nothing marked. Especially this time of year. When I say that it's off the grid, that's an understatement. It's not as much *off* the grid as *allergic* to the grid. I didn't actually know that anybody lived there full-time. But the Delaney family does. Has for a while, it turns out."

"This doesn't sound like a story with a happy ending," Ramona said quietly. "And I know I've told you this before, but those are the stories that I prefer."

He nodded. "I hear you. We got out there and we found what I can only describe as a collection of shacks. There's no running water. They're living off camp stoves if they're fancy, and campfires if not. It's not clear who is actually a member of the family and who is… just out there, for fun, I guess?"

"Some people like to live like that." Ramona had seen this firsthand in her time here. There were those who came to these wild places to disappear, and they pursued that goal no matter what it cost them in comfort or ease. "They don't want to answer to anyone, or do anything they don't want to do. Ever. On some level, I can see why that's appealing."

"I like running water," Knox said, his mouth curving. It seemed to be connected directly to the center of her, like a kind of punch. And everywhere else. "Radiant floor heating. Electrical appliances. Me, personally, I'm of the opinion that modern advances make life better rather than worse. I like camping as much as the next guy, but I'm always happy to come back home."

"I love getting away from everything," Ramona agreed. "My grandfather and I used to go on long camping trips in the summers down in Yellowstone and over near Big Sky. He taught me how to forage, how to fend for myself, how to build myself a shelter in any kind of weather. All life skills that I'm happy to have."

Knox waited, like he knew where she was going with this.

She smiled. "But I'm with you. I like coming home. I don't really think you would appreciate getting away from it all if you didn't have the contrast of it." She made a face. "Also, for the most part, my observation is that most of the people you're describing who live in situations like that aren't really doing it because freedom calls. It's usually because they're avoiding pesky inconveniences like law enforcement."

"Atticus confirmed that."

He traced a few patterns on the table, idly, and she found herself wondering what he was drawing. Or, if it was letters, what they spelled out. She didn't let herself ask.

"I'm not going to lie," Knox said into the quiet of the kitchen. "It wasn't the most welcoming place I've ever been. Happily, Boone is intimidating without trying. And Wilder can talk to anyone. So we didn't get shot, which is a bonus. It looked dicey there for a minute."

Both the doctor and the woman in her had to *work* not to respond to that. Not to ask what he meant by *dicey*—but then, she could guess.

"It doesn't sound like you found who you were looking for, either," she said instead, because the less she imagined *dicey*, the better.

"They definitely didn't like anyone coming there, looking for one of them," Knox agreed, and he laughed. "They also strenuously discouraged us from ever doing that again."

"I'm sorry that you wasted your time." She cupped her hands around her mug because otherwise, she didn't think she'd be able to keep from reaching over and touching him.

"Though I suppose I'm glad that you went, if only so I know to avoid that area. Something I probably would have done anyway, given the name. My experience of Western place names is that they tell harsh and sometimes bitter truths."

"That they do." Knox took another drink of his coffee, and continued his story. "We figured they knew exactly where Shoshana was, but there wasn't much use trying to get such fine, upstanding folks to share that information with us under the circumstances. We figured we'd regroup, maybe see if we could happen upon one of them the next time they came into town. Because they'll have to every once in a while. Everybody does."

"Great thinking," Ramona said dryly. "They sound like exactly the kind of people who would react well to being ambushed at the General Store."

"Fair point," he agreed, his eyes crinkling in the corners. "Anyway, when you're leaving Devil's Gorge, you have to sort of maneuver around this big boulder to find your way back out of the gorge and onto one of the so-called roads. It separates you from the part with all the scarily rundown shacks with piles of debris all around them and the folks who look a whole lot like serial killers, waving their weapons."

"This is sounding better and better."

He fully grinned at her then, his eyes gleaming like burnished gold, and Ramona felt her breath flutter in her chest.

Making it abundantly clear to her that she wasn't *clean* when it came to him. At all.

But he kept going. Thank God. "There was a girl waiting and she flagged us down. She couldn't have been more than eighteen. She knew exactly who I was, though I've never met her before and she refused to tell us her name. What she did tell us is that Shoshana is in Billings. She even gave us an address."

That could only be a good thing, Ramona thought, though there was a part of her that didn't want Shoshana found—because what would that mean for little Hailey. And Knox, who she'd watched dote on that little girl in a way she wasn't sure she'd known he could.

But she didn't want to say that out loud.

"Please don't tell me that you left that poor girl there," Ramona said instead. "That doesn't sound like the sort of place where eighteen-year-old girls should be hanging out."

Knox nodded. "A sentiment that was widely shared between me and my brothers. But the thing is, Ramona, you can't go around kidnapping eighteen-year-old girls. No matter how much you might think they'd benefit from it. It's pretty universally frowned upon."

Ramona frowned. "I guess that's true. But I don't like it."

"Neither do I." His gaze was serious. "But taking her with us wasn't an option, believe me. I think she might have shot us herself if we'd tried."

They sat there, then. It was quiet in the kitchen. She had been reading a book on the couch and there was music playing softly from the other room—one of her favorite songs about alchemy. A little too on the nose, Ramona thought, because *she* wasn't the one who went around denying the alchemy in the first place—

But it did not do her any good to think about any lingering *alchemy* between herself and this man. Just like it didn't do her any good to jump to conclusions about why he was here at ten o'clock at night, sharing these things with her.

He could have texted.

Or, given the state of their relationship these days, he could have kept her out of the loop entirely.

"I'm hoping you're not here to tell me that you lost two of your brothers to the mountains," Ramona said instead of launching into a monologue on *alchemy*. Or, worse, their relationship.

She knew better than to make speeches to him. The last time she had, she'd told him she loved him and that had resulted in her having to stop all things Knox Carey. Cold turkey.

"They're good," Knox assured her. "We started back, but it was already dark and rapidly getting much too icy. We figured we were better off not trying to drive all the way back. So we went north and spent the night out at that ridiculously fancy Resort at Ransom Ridge instead."

Ramona blinked. "I didn't see that coming. I would have thought that the entire Carey family stood stoutly against luxury resorts of all kinds. Purely on principle."

The Resort at Ransom Ridge wasn't just *fancy*. It was a world-class five-star *experience*. It catered to high-flyers, who could literally take a helicopter or their private planes in, thereby sparing themselves the indignity of mountain roads and the vagaries of the small towns along the way. It had existed in hotel form while Ramona was growing up. But it had skyrocketed into the luxury space over the course of the past fifteen years or so, and was now considered one of the finest resort experiences in the Rocky Mountains—and the world, having been named a three Michelin key hotel last year.

Knox laughed again. "Some members of the Carey family stand against almost anything that's new," he agreed. "The thing about the Resort at Ransom Ridge is that it isn't new. That family has been around forever."

He leaned forward, in storytelling mode, and that did not exactly help her keep her heart in one piece. "They all sprang up out there after an outlaw hightailed it out of Livingston in the wake of a botched bank robbery and a shootout. Knowing them to be about as ornery as possible, I bet they decided to make it all fancy and elegant to spite him. That's the kind of people they are."

Knox grinned. "And being a hardheaded Montanan myself, I support it."

"I heard the rooms there start at nearly a grand a night," Ramona said, shaking her head. "In the off-season. Which this is not."

"It helps to know people," Knox said. "But yes, we went from the Delaney off-grid shack situation to the epitome of Western high life, and I'm not sure that Boone will ever recover." He shrugged. "Wilder and I were fine."

"You have hardier constitutions when it comes to the finer things." Ramona laughed. "Or so I've heard."

Knox nodded, and then he spread his hands out on the table, staring down at them like he didn't know what to do with them. Like he was considering putting them on Ramona, maybe, but didn't.

She could relate.

She needed to *stop* relating.

"There was some weather to wait out before we drove back today," Knox continued after a moment. "It took us a good while. I dropped my brothers off at the ranch, checked in on Hailey and my mom, and then figured I should come down into town and do a little brainstorming with Atticus about my next move. Then I figured I might as well eat, because I was hungry. And since I was already here, I thought I'd fill you in on what happened."

Ramona searched his face. Her heart was beating a little too fast, still, though she was doing her best to ignore it.

With about as much luck as before.

Meaning, none.

"You're going to have to go to Billings, right?" she asked him. "I feel like there's no way forward with anything until you know what's going on with poor Shoshana." She flushed a little after she said that. "I don't know why I'm assuming she's *poor Shoshana*, but I am. I can't help it."

Knox was watching her, that brooding, intense look on his face again. And she'd never been any good at resisting that face. "I want you to come with me, Ramona."

She felt her heart stutter a bit. It was like everything suddenly froze, then clattered. She swallowed, and realized her throat was tight.

And it was so easy—too easy—to simply go along with this. To let him in. To talk with him like this, like he often came here and updated her on his life, with all their clothes on. To laugh, and feel cozy in this kitchen, like he belonged here.

But that wasn't their story.

She could understand why he'd called her on Christmas Eve. It was what he'd said at the time—he'd called the clinic line, because he was calling the doctor. Because there was an abandoned infant in the mix who'd been exposed to the elements for an indeterminate amount of time, and that was a perfectly reasonable thing for him to do.

This was something else.

Ramona could see that he knew it. She could see it all over his face. It was there in that brooding intensity. He knew that this was a big ask because this wasn't a medical inquiry.

This was personal.

And Ramona had to caution herself, because her urge

was always to simply jump in and try to fix things. To say *yes*, immediately, because that was what she wanted in the moment—but it didn't actually get her what she *really* wanted, in the end.

She'd made a lot of assumptions about what they both knew, what they both felt, what they both were doing, and they'd still ended up apart.

Ramona had still ended up with her heart broken into smithereens, and if nothing else, she owed it to herself not to throw herself into a whole new heartbreak all over again.

Knox was looking at her expectantly. Maybe a little apprehensively, which she thought was only appropriate.

He was waiting for her to answer.

So she did. She blew out a breath, and then she held his gaze with hers, direct and intent.

Because this time she wasn't going to assume a damned thing.

What she said instead was, "Why?"

Chapter Seven

KNOX WAS NOT expecting the question.

His throat was strangely dry. His chest felt tight.

"It feels right that we do this together," he said, and he meant it, but then he heard those words hanging in the air.

Ramona didn't change expression. Still, Knox found himself reacting as if she had.

He sat up straighter. "I know that sounds ridiculous. But you were there on Christmas Eve. You were there with us, with me, for days. I feel like we're both invested in Hailey and also Shoshana, and it just felt right to ask you if you wanted to be part of this, too."

He didn't know why he felt like he'd just ran a marathon, a supposed life goal he'd achieved exactly once in college and never needed to try again. He thought he might be sweating. Possibly he was a little bit lightheaded.

Meanwhile, Ramona looked like some kind of goddess of light tonight, and that was not really helpful at keeping him relaxed. She had braided her hair on one side, and it hung over her shoulder, all of those shades of gold seeming to gleam here in her happy apartment that always seemed to have its own glow. She was wearing leggings, thick wool socks, and a big, oversized sweatshirt that he knew felt like a cloud to the touch. He also knew that she wasn't wearing a bra beneath it, which was information his body did not need to have right now.

All she did was gaze back at him, looking irritatingly serene while he felt like he was coming apart.

"Why?" she asked again.

Knox felt something like panic work its way through him. Because this was not how things normally went with them.

Ramona did not melt and come to him, as he'd expected she would. She didn't look like she was even considering it.

Usually, it didn't take much for her to decide the distance between them was too much. She would normally make that move—sometimes emotionally, sometimes impatiently. She would kiss him. Maybe come over and sit on his lap. Reach out and put her hands on him. *Something.*

And he'd known that she was doing these things, of course. He hadn't been blind to the way things were between them. Though Knox was pretty sure that until *this* very moment, he hadn't really understood how much he relied on her inability to resist him.

He'd known that she was avoiding him these past two months. She'd told him that she never wanted to see him again, and she'd held to that for a lot longer than usual. They had never been apart more than a week since they'd met until she'd called it off in October.

Knox had admired her resolve. And he'd been determined to do his part, if that was what she wanted. He hadn't sought her out directly. He hadn't gone where he knew he'd find her, so he could "accidentally" bump into her. He had not made sure that she would see him somewhere in town. It was a point of some shame, in fact, that before he'd done all of that and more.

So you can always claim you weren't involved, it just happened, it was all me, she'd said the last time they'd talked in October. *Plausible deniability until it chokes you, right, Knox?*

But it hadn't dawned on him that she could hold onto that resistance in person.

He ran his hands over his face. "Today my mom asked me how I made it through Christmas Eve and the storm with the baby. When I told her that I called you, she pointed out that it's very telling who a person calls first when they really need help. Maybe that's why I'm here tonight. Just..." She only waited, her gaze expectant. His throat was so dry he was almost convinced he was coming down with some hideous virus. "You're the person I always want to call, Ramona. The person I want to tell things to. The only person I could think of taking to Billings to do this thing I'm not sure I want to do."

He saw something flash in her gaze, but he couldn't read it. She'd always been like that. She had always been remarkably unreadable when she wanted. She had a better poker face than anyone else he knew and she could maintain it pretty much forever.

It's a clinical necessity, she'd told him once. *Doctors can't have reactions all over their faces when patients tell them deeply personal or embarrassing things.*

I'm not your patient, he'd replied, and then he'd kissed her until she was flushed and smiling and his.

That poker face of hers had always had the same, very specific effect on him. It still did.

He wanted to find his way beneath it by any means necessary. And usually, the means he'd chosen had led to them both naked and coming apart at the seams.

She sat there across the table from him now, studying him, as if she was thinking about what he'd said about being his first call. She tilted her head slightly to one side, so that the braid dipped down even lower, and he had to order himself not to reach across the table to tug on it, maybe wrap it around his fist and then pull her close.

It felt like an actual, physical pain that he couldn't. That he didn't.

"I won't pretend that I don't like hearing that," she told him, when he'd begun to think that she didn't intend to speak again tonight and then what would he do? "But again, Knox, I have to ask." She shrugged, a little helplessly, he thought. Or maybe he was mistaking that helplessness, because there was definitely a challenge in the way she was looking at him. "Why?"

Knox felt that panicked sensation inside him tighten, and

then, when he thought it might actually strangle him where he sat, he began to feel instead like a spool of thread unraveling. Rapidly. And there didn't seem to be a single thing he could do to stop it.

The way she was looking at him wasn't without some compassion, but that made it worse.

"I don't know," he managed to say.

He thought he saw a hint of a smile on her face, but it was gone in a moment. "I think that you do."

Maybe he was having a heart attack. Or maybe he just *wanted* to have a heart attack, because then his favorite doctor would have to put her hands on him.

Still, Knox also understood what she was doing here. Or he thought he did.

Ramona wasn't going to make this easy on him. Not this time. She'd been easy on him for too long. She'd let him claim that he was all about the honesty, but that was never really put to the test, was it?

Because she always gave him another chance. She was the one woman he couldn't charm, or maybe the only one he didn't try to charm. That hadn't been true at first, of course. At first it had been nothing but charm and heat and as close to giddy as Knox thought he'd ever been.

But over the course of the year and a half since she'd arrived in town, since they'd started going back and forth, he knew perfectly well that he'd stopped worrying about charming her. He hadn't defaulted to his usual little act to keep things running smoothly.

And he knew why.

He'd *wanted* her to wash her hands of him. He'd *wanted* her to take him seriously when he told her this thing between them was never going to go anywhere. That it was better not to get too attached.

She'd seen him with his mask off every time. He'd wanted that.

And she had accepted him completely, which he could not for even one moment imagine he deserved.

Hell, he knew he didn't.

Ramona had accepted him. She'd *loved* him, no matter what kind of asshole he was, and what had he done in return? Each and every time she'd tried to raise the topic of what was happening between them, he'd shut it down.

Like it would have killed him to concede that yes, he'd always known that he didn't intend to stay in Cowboy Point. And yes, he'd never wanted any kind of entanglement to get in the way of his leaving.

But, also yes, this thing between them had ended up in much deeper water than he'd anticipated.

Right now, he couldn't think of a single good reason why he hadn't said those things at least once, even though he knew his own rationale backwards and forwards and to the point that it sometimes drove even him crazy.

But it shook something in him that she wasn't going to take the lead now, the way she always had before. She wasn't going to give him so much as a hint of that plausible deniability. Ramona had let him in, but she was clearly perfectly content to sit here and watch him spin in the wind.

The worst part of that was that he knew he had it coming.

It was like he could hear his father in his head, then. His larger-than-life father, who he'd never imagined *could* die and still hadn't accepted would. And likely soon—

Knox couldn't let himself think about that now.

So really, son, drawled the Zeke in his head, *what it boils down to is whether or not you're a coward.*

Because a coward would pretend he didn't know what was happening here and leave everything the way it was. Out of the same fear that had gotten him here in the first place.

Knox had never considered himself cowardly before. Not out on the football field, not academically, not with his business ventures. In fact, the only thing he could point to in his entire life that might fit that definition was the way he'd acted with Ramona since he'd met her, because she had taken him completely by surprise.

He hadn't *wanted* to meet a woman who could make him want to change his whole life.

Truth was, he still didn't. But he couldn't live with himself if he didn't get up and do something to prove that whatever else might happen, he wasn't *only* the plausible deniability guy.

The wildest part of that was that even as he sat there

thinking this, he still felt as if the chair at her kitchen table was holding him in place.

Which, even in his own head, sounded a lot like some increasingly weak excuses.

But he'd been too restless to stay home when he'd gotten back there today. And yes, he'd wanted to talk to Atticus, but he could have called the deputy sheriff just as easily.

Of course you should go down to Cowboy Point, his mother had said in what was, looking back at it, an alarmingly serene tone of voice. When Belinda was not known for her smoothness of temper. *I'm sure you have any number of things to take care of.*

Knox had kissed his sweet little Hailey on her forehead, and then on her nose because she was so cute and she made her little noises at him, and then he'd gone.

To talk to Atticus, he'd told himself. But he'd known the whole time that he would end up here.

Really it came down to the advice Zeke had given all his sons at one point or another. *Shit or get off the pot.*

Simple and to the point, a lot like Zeke himself.

Knox took a breath, straight into that place near his solar plexus where he still felt like he was coming apart. And he comforted himself with the knowledge that no matter what happened now, no matter if he really did put himself out there for once with her, he couldn't make their situation *more* messed up.

It was oddly cheering.

He moved then, and then had to admit that it felt good to watch her eyes go wide. As if she'd expected him to do something even less than he already had.

That stung.

But it didn't stop him.

He thought there might have to be a reckoning at some point, to figure out why it was that he had no fear at all strolling into Devil's Gorge where literally anything could have happened to him and no one would ever have found his remains, but a little bit of vulnerability scared the hell out of him.

But even as he thought that, standing beside the table, looking down into Ramona's unfathomably pretty face, he knew the answer.

The love in his family came with a whole lot of mockery, and Knox had long ago decided that he was never going to let them *see* that they got to him. Not as the youngest. He already got the worst of it. If they knew they bothered him, it would have been worse. They couldn't help themselves.

He didn't know when it had turned into a cage he didn't know how to get out of.

Ramona wasn't his family. And vulnerability with her would never become a joke the way it would with his brothers, because that wasn't who she was.

Maybe he'd known that all along.

Maybe he'd known that if he was going to go in at all, he'd have to go all the way.

There's no maybe *about it,* he told himself then.

But he was getting ahead of himself. He wasn't going anywhere, in or out in any other direction. He was still just standing here, *looking* at her.

Knox reached down into that place that felt like it was unspooling, and decided that if there was a way out of the cage he hadn't understood he was in until now—this was it.

And it felt a lot like it was now or never.

He moved around the table and knelt down beside her chair. That put him just about at eye level—though because he was on his knees, she had to look down at him a bit.

This close, he could not only hear but see it when she sucked in a breath. He could also see the beginnings of that flush he loved to watch roll out over her skin like a quiet, rosy thunderstorm.

She didn't say anything. She also didn't ask him *why* again, so he took that as a victory.

He put his hands on her legs and he didn't crack a smile.

Because this was Ramona, and the mask was off, and anyway, this was serious.

"You've always gotten this wrong," he told her, his voice low, maybe, but intent. "I know you think I don't feel anything. Or I do, but I don't want to, which amounts to the same thing. But that's not it. Of course I feel. I feel all the things that you do. I just never wanted you to think that this was going places I knew it wouldn't go." She didn't react to that. And her legs were warm in those leggings beneath his palms, and touching her was still the best thing he could think of. He felt something beating in him, like some kind of drum, urging him on. "I was trying to protect you."

It was a testament, maybe, to the intensity of the moment that she didn't laugh at that. *Scoff* at it, more like. Because he could see a gleam of that sort of thing in her gaze.

He kept going, because there was no turning back now. "I love my family. I love the ranch. I love Montana. But I never wanted anything more than my family time here. I never wanted anything to tie me down at all. I figured the best way to go about that was to be brutally honest about that from the start. Not just with you. With everyone."

For the first time in years, he thought about his high school girlfriend. He'd heard she'd met a nice guy and had moved to Denver, and he liked that for her.

Because he'd broken her heart, too.

"You certainly succeeded," Ramona told him. And her voice was as calm as ever, but there was something a little more turbulent in all that blue in her eyes. "You have always been the very soul of brutal honesty."

That wasn't a compliment, he was well aware.

"Ramona." He moved a little closer and tugged her around on her chair so she was facing him. So he was staring right into her face. Her astonishingly beautiful face that only got prettier closer in. "We were never supposed to meet when we did. I wasn't even supposed to be here."

He shook his head, but he didn't stop. "I was planning

to break it to my parents on Easter that I was done with the ranch for the moment. I had it all planned out. I was going to go on a road trip, first and foremost. Take a look at this country of ours myself, not through a screen. I was going to pick a place to settle and see how I liked it. But instead, my dad told us…"

Knox broke off. He blew out a breath. "How could I leave with my dad sick? I couldn't. I couldn't even consider it. And now there's Hailey. My name on a birth certificate and a little baby girl who doesn't seem to have anyone. And the whole while, between those two things, there's been you."

Ramona was tense beneath his hands. Her eyes were darker than usual.

But when she spoke again, her voice was as maddeningly smooth and even as ever.

"Yes," she said, coolly, "life does happen while you're busy pretending it hasn't started yet. A thousand apologies for not making it easier on you. By… not moving here, I guess? Not going to find food on my first night? I don't know what I was thinking."

"If I was going to stay here, you must know that I would have locked you down already, Ramona," he belted out. "I knew you were trouble that very first night. Haven't I made that clear?"

She leaned a little closer, so that her gaze was practically inside of him, tearing him to shreds. "The only thing you've ever made clear is that every single thing I feel about you is my problem, not yours."

"Yeah," he said gruffly. "I think you know that's bullshit."

Ramona stared at him. She didn't melt. She didn't cry.

She stared at him, and he had the terrible, paralyzing thought he'd left it too late after all, and that was nobody's fault but his—

But then, barely an inch from his face, she blinked, and he saw the gleam he recognized in all that blue. That softening he sure as hell didn't deserve, but he'd take it.

Knox wasn't sure he'd ever felt this kind of relief in his life.

When he finally leaned in and kissed her again, after the two longest months of his life without her, it felt like fire.

And better yet, like coming home.

Chapter Eight

RAMONA COULDN'T KEEP herself from answering the phone when Knox called, or letting him in when he showed up, so really—kissing him was a foregone conclusion.

And just like every time he kissed her, he turned her completely inside out.

It had always been like this. His mouth on hers was immediately carnal, almost unbearably intense.

It was everything.

He ate at her mouth, and one of his big, callused hands moved to cup her cheek so he could guide her mouth as he kissed her. Like this was the first time.

Like they needed a beginners' manual to figure out this chemistry when it had been nothing but explosive from the start.

She wrapped her arms around his neck and then he was moving. He lifted her up, still kissing her, so he could slide his hands beneath the cozy sweatshirt she wore. It was like he needed to reacquaint himself with her shape, or her skin, or maybe he was matching the memories he'd been carrying around to the reality.

Ramona couldn't pretend she wasn't doing the exact same thing. She pressed into him, because the wall of his chest was a kind of glory—hard and hot—and she'd believed she would never touch him again. She had vowed she wouldn't.

And it was true that it felt lovely and intimate to sit around fully clothed with this man, sharing a bit of quiet together.

But the minute they touched, they incinerated.

Knox made a low, growling noise that had never once failed to connect directly to the greedy place between her legs that she sometimes thought had been made just for him.

And she didn't know if she jumped or he hauled her up, but either way, she wrapped her legs around his waist and then he was carrying her.

But they didn't make it far.

They never did.

He crossed out of the kitchen and into the living room, but then he stopped so he could hold her up against the nearest wall, and they stayed like that for a good, long while.

Knox got that sweatshirt up and off of her, but it took too long. They had to slam their mouths together again and lick their way inside, angling their heads to make it better, to make up for it.

They had to do that until it became necessary to breathe.

He moved so he could lean back a little, but he kept her legs in place around him. Ramona pressed her shoulder blades into the wall, because she knew what he wanted.

She wanted it too.

He wore a dark, glittering, intensely possessive look on his face as he smoothed his palms over her breasts. She was now completely bared to him from the waist up, and she could see how much he liked it.

She did too, especially when he began to play.

Though his version of play made her buck her hips against him, pressing herself as best she could against the heat of him. And better still, that hard, heavy ridge in his jeans that she knew was all for her.

"Do you know how hard it was to keep my hands off you for days beneath my roof?" he asked her, in that dark voice of his that made her shiver, everywhere.

"I hope it was torture," she managed to get out as she arched her back to give him better access. "I hope it hurt."

"You know that it did."

Knox slid his hands around to grip her shoulder blades and then he lifted her straight up, so he could tease her nipple and suck it into his hot mouth.

And he broke her apart that easily, with one sharp, hard tug. It felt like lightning racing through her, crashing down, making her throw her head back while her whole body convulsed.

He only laughed, his mouth still too hot and she could feel it too well, and that made it go on longer. When she started to come down a little, he devoted himself to her other breast, sending her spinning all over again.

Knox pulled her away from the wall and spun around, and then they were down on their knees on her soft, plush, off-white rug. It was thick and cozy and was spread out before the greatest indulgence in this apartment. Her electric fireplace that she could turn on and off with the click of a button, rather than heaving about in the cold with axes and wood.

That is an abomination, Knox had said the first time he'd seen it. And though he'd been shaking his head, there'd been laughter in his eyes.

There's a reason most lumberjacks are men, Ramona had replied. *It's about time, labor, and upper body strength differentials, but mostly I just want to be cozy.*

He had rolled his eyes then and every other time he'd come here and found it crackling away in all of its electric glory. But he had to admit that it kept the house warm.

Which he didn't seem to mind when he was doing the kinds of things he was doing now. Like peeling off her socks and leggings, then her panties. And taking his time as he did it, as if he was marveling over her body for the very first time.

"It's been too damned long since I've tasted you," he growled at her.

He laid her out before him, without a single scrap of clothes on her body. Then he found his way between her legs so he could hook her knees over his shoulders.

Then he settled down on his forearms, slid his hands under her butt, and proceeded to make her shatter.

Over and over and over again.

This was only one of the terrible things about Knox Carey.

There were many. But the utter, easy delight he took in licking into her, tasting her, indulging himself in her, was quite possibly the very worst.

No wonder she was addicted. No wonder she'd found the need to create sobriety programs to try to keep herself on the straight and narrow where he was concerned.

The man was dangerous. He seemed to know the things her own body could do whether she knew it herself or not. He used his mouth like it was a weapon and a love song, and he coaxed her over that edge again and again.

He used his talented fingers to play with her, to tease her. He thrust deep inside of her with one finger, then two, finding that spot there on the inside and then using it against her—deliberately making her scream.

And she knew better than to tell him she couldn't take any more, because he always seemed to see that as a challenge.

A challenge he had yet to lose.

Tonight he proceeded to show her why and how he would always win. Until she was limp and half laughing, half sobbing there before the fire. He kissed his way up her torso, lavishing attention everywhere. From her inner thigh to her navel. From one hip bone to the other. This time, when he found her breasts, he kissed them and left her shivering, slightly, as sensation wound its way through her.

But when he got to her face again, he only smiled. He took his time kissing her, and then he rolled to his feet.

Then he simply picked her up off the floor, hoisting her up in his arms as if she weighed about as much as one of the throw pillows.

Ramona wasn't a giant of a woman, but she'd hit five foot eight in the sixth grade. She wasn't tiny, either.

Yet Knox always made her feel as if she was a precious little object he could tuck away in his pocket and keep safe, if she liked.

Ramona had always liked.

She snuggled into him as he carried her, breathing in that scent of his. No longer the cold night he'd brought with him when he'd come to her door, but his particular scent that she knew as well as she knew her own.

Now she also knew what it was like for her own body to smell entirely like him. When she'd taken a shower here in her own home, this morning, she'd felt a strange pang of something a lot like grief when she'd come out of the shower, dried herself off, and realized that she had washed away the spicy fragrance of his shampoo. The bold notes of his soap, like pine sap and rich earth.

She could smell that on him now, in the warm crook of his neck, but beneath that there was the scent that was just *him.* And something else that always made her think of towering mountains, braced against the endless sky. There was something *expansive* about inhaling this man.

It made her feel as if she was both tiny in his arms and at least a hundred times her own size inside.

He carried her into the bedroom, and, once again, she was so happy that she'd converted this upstairs space. When she'd arrived it had been little more than a few jumbled attic rooms someone had tried to throw together into an apartment for her grandfather's carer in his last days.

It had been chilly and unwelcoming and, frankly, depressing. She didn't know who had lived up here, but she doubted very much that they'd enjoyed it.

Now the main bedroom was a festival of soft, inviting ease. She had a king-size bed and thick rugs to keep her feet from being cold when she walked around. She had a cozy reading nook and an office area behind a glass door—a former closet—where she could do actual work if she liked. All this and a view of Dallas Lisle's mountain lighthouse on the far ridge in front of her, rising up like a beacon of hope and folly at once.

The bed was piled high with softness. Layers of linens, comforters, pillows. The first time Knox had seen her bedroom, months after the first time they'd gotten together downstairs on an air mattress, he had actually stopped and stared.

I'm not sure men are allowed in a place like this, he'd said with a laugh. *It feels like some kind of temple.*

They shouldn't be allowed, she'd agreed, but then she'd smiled. She'd taken his hands and pushed him back into the particular cloudlike softness of her specially selected mattress, and her previously most dangerous addiction, that being bedding that could give Michelin-rated resorts a run for their money.

He might have been a tough cowboy, but he'd been an immediate convert.

And now he lay her in the middle of all that frothy, airy featherdown sweetness. Knox didn't move his gaze from her as he shrugged out of the flannel shirt he was wearing and the long-sleeved T-shirt beneath it. Then he shoved off the rest of his clothes like they were in his way, leaving his jeans and his long johns and his winter socks in a pile on the floor.

Then he crawled toward her, his eyes gold with intent. And he was so wired into her that she felt his gaze like a shower of sparks beneath her skin.

And Ramona thought about the vows she'd made—and had broken repeatedly already, out there in her living room. In her kitchen before that.

She'd been holding the line that it was touching him that made the difference, but she supposed she'd known all along that she was splitting hairs.

And now she felt soft and destroyed and molten hot, and he was coming toward her with that burning hot promise all over him.

Ramona knew that if she had any self-respect at all that she would shut this down. Right now before it went any further.

She knew it, but there wasn't one single part of her that wanted to do that. There wasn't the faintest hint of any resistance inside of her.

Instead, she thought about the things he'd said, out there in the kitchen, showing her more of himself than she thought he ever had before. And maybe more important, the things that she thought he'd *wanted* to say, but couldn't.

Ramona had beat herself up for that a thousand times. Interpreting his silence as admission, when maybe it was really just him not having anything to say.

But she didn't believe that was true. She didn't truly believe that she was so delusional that she would make up what she saw in him.

She followed her intuition in her work all the time. She was an excellent diagnostician, so why had she convinced herself that she could read pretty much any human being on this planet except him?

But she knew the answer. He hadn't responded to her the way she'd wanted him to—the way she needed him to. It was easier to tell herself he felt nothing at all than to sit in the pain of thinking that he felt all the same things, but for some reason wouldn't step into them the way she did.

The truth of this, she knew with the same certainty she'd felt that first night so long ago, was that she was in love with him.

It had grabbed her that fast, and it had never released its grip.

But she also thought—and had for some time, though tonight cinched it for her—that he loved her.

No matter what he did or didn't say, did or didn't do, or how it all made her feel.

It hadn't escaped her notice that he'd put her on the same level as the father she knew that he adored and the baby he clearly felt responsible for now.

Maybe what she needed to do was redefine her responses to a situation that she was beginning to think she'd been misreading all along.

What did it matter what they called themselves? What did it matter what he thought his future ought to look like when he was making no move toward it? What did it matter if he never spouted her poetry?

Maybe the two of them were the poem.

She'd looked up from a local beer that the Bennett sisters who ran Mountain Mama Pizza had told her they'd imported from Flintworks, a local brewery down in Marietta. She'd thought the local IPA would be the hero of the evening, but then she'd looked up.

Knox had been there and her heart hadn't belonged to her ever since.

Now, on the other side of so many months of back and forth, he'd admitted that there hadn't been anyone else for him, either.

Did she really need a bigger declaration than that?

He stretched out beside her and propped his head on his hand. "You look serious," he said.

"I'm always serious," she replied. "I'm a doctor."

Then she smiled and crawled on top of him.

And finally, it was her turn to play.

She had yet to find a single square inch of this man's body that she didn't love, but that didn't keep her from looking. Ramona took her time making sure she hadn't gotten any part of him wrong in her memories.

But when she kissed and licked her way down that outrageously rich and gorgeous chest of his, following the dark hair that led to the part of him that made her mouth water, he hauled her up again.

"Not now," he said, with a particular wickedness in his gaze that thrilled her. "I'm too hungry."

He rolled her over and gathered her to him, so he could reach down and pull one of her knees up high. Then he was there between them, that silken steel of his finally rubbing into all of her white-hot softness.

"If you really haven't slept with anyone else—" she began.

"I haven't. I'm not a liar, Ramona."

She smoothed her fingers over the place where a frown was introducing itself between his eyes. "That wasn't an accusation. I only wanted to tell you that we don't need a condom. Not for me. You know I'm on the pill."

And she didn't say the rest—that maybe she hadn't trusted that he *wasn't* sleeping with other people the last year and a half, because he'd maintained that either one of them could do that at any time.

He looked almost stricken, for a moment.

"In case it wasn't clear, I haven't slept with anyone else either, Knox," Ramona said, distinctly. Had she not told him that directly? She couldn't remember. "I thought you knew that."

His breath seemed to leave him in a rush. She could see emotion in that bright gaze of his, but then his mouth was on hers, his hands on her face again because he liked to keep her jaw where he wanted it. Because what he wanted was to practically eat her alive.

And even as he did that, he was moving his hips and finding his way—but not fast enough.

Ramona reached down between them and wrapped her hand as best she could around the thick width of him, then guided him inside of her at last.

At last.

But he still wasn't moving fast enough for her, so she threw her legs around his hips and pressed her heels against his butt, then slammed him home.

They both groaned.

Because it had always been this hot. It had always been the same almost too tight fit for one breath. Another. Then he moved, and she met that movement, and it tipped over into pure, impossible heat.

Only this time, there was no barrier between them.

It was only him.

That great, big, hard length of him as he began to move. As he tested this magical fit, sinking inside of her so very slowly, then pulling back out again.

So slowly she began to quiver. So slowly that she thought she might die.

"Please…" she whispered.

And he laughed, because he knew.

He always knew.

But he picked up the pace.

And it was all about the way he thrust deep and the way she met that thrust. They rolled over and over on the soft bed, and maybe she bit him on his shoulder. Maybe the grip he had on her hips left marks.

None of that mattered.

It was like they were fighting—to get close enough that they could slip their skins entirely and become one.

Anything to chase that fire until it burned them both enough that they couldn't tell where one of them stopped and the other began.

Somewhere in there, she stopped pretending that she could control the pace. She stopped pretending that she could control him either. And then there was only that wild, restless rush to the edge.

Until he finally thrust deep enough that it sent her flying, and he leaped out into the same stretch of starshine behind her.

She felt him scald her, deep inside, and found herself shattering all over again almost before she finished the first go-round.

He was murmuring her name in disbelief, and wonder, again and again, as they scattered into too many pieces to count.

And they fell asleep like that, him inside her, her body wrapped around him.

Sometime in the night, they woke up and did it all over again. This time it seemed almost more urgent, as if they couldn't believe they'd woken up in the same bed again.

Later still, Ramona woke up to hear the shower running. She crawled out of the warm bed and went into her pretty little bathroom to join him there, and she couldn't keep herself from smiling when she stepped into the shower stall.

He kissed her again and again by way of a greeting, and then she'd nestled into him as the shower came down all over them.

And it made her heart feel like it was singing.

In the morning, he woke up insatiable, but she was even hungrier. So Ramona crawled on top of him and went up on her knees, then sat herself down on him. She took all of him, thick and long, until she felt so full of him that she was surprised her body didn't break open.

She braced her hands on Knox's hard chest and she

leaned over him as she began to lift herself up and settle down on him again. Her hair fell all around them like a kind of curtain, but she could still see him.

And all that intensity in his golden gaze.

His hands gripped her hips and his gaze stayed on hers. And he let her ride him at her own lazy, then frantic pace, until they both shouted out their explosive finish within seconds of each other.

It was so good, Ramona thought, that it was no wonder it hurt.

When they finally got out of bed, it felt painful to tear herself away from him but she managed it. She wrapped herself up in his flannel and pulled on her heavy socks. Then she went into her kitchen and blinked in the morning light, then made them a big, hearty breakfast of eggs and toast and sausages—all bought from a local farmer she knew by name.

She still got a kick out of that.

They sat in the kitchen the same way they had last night, but Ramona felt that everything was different. They were different. That everything had changed.

And she did not remind herself that she had felt this way before. More than once.

That was the old Ramona. The new Ramona was going to live in the freaking present, even if it killed her.

When they finished eating, Knox did the dishes. They showered and got dressed again—though they were both a little too tempted to delay things a little longer.

Once again, it hurt to deny herself.

It really didn't get better with time.

Knox held her hand as they walked away from the temptation of her bed and went down the stairs, and she pretended it didn't make her feel butterflies in her stomach. When they got to his truck, he lifted her hand to his mouth and kissed it.

Ramona couldn't breathe. She wasn't sure she wanted to.

She leaned in and kissed him back, then they climbed into his truck, and headed out toward Billings.

Where there would be answers, Ramona hoped. Of one sort or another.

And she would be there with him no matter what.

Chapter Nine

IT WAS AN easy couple of hours to Billings. The hardest part was getting down Copper Mountain without sliding off of it, but that was always true. The road the locals liked to call Desolation Drive was treacherous even in summer. Once they made it down the mountain in one piece, the drive from Marietta to Livingston and on to the interstate was a breeze.

Montana was used to its winter storms. And though the drive east was snowy, the road was clear. They reached Billings by midmorning.

Knox had always liked Billings. As they drove into the biggest city in the state, he saw flashy signs for the sporting goods chain that was owned by Billy Grey, the brother of Jason Grey who owned and still ran the bar at Grey's Saloon in the center of Marietta. It was kind of like when he'd been looking for property to buy up by Flathead Lake and he'd kept running into the influence of Jonah Flint, who had a big spread up that way. Jonah was the twin brother of Jasper Flint, who'd opened Knox's favorite microbrewery, Flint-works, in the old Marietta train depot, while he was busy romancing the woman who was now his wife. And the mayor.

There were Marietta connections everywhere, and even though Knox and his family were Cowboy Point people going back to the community's founding as a mining camp, he claimed Marietta as his own too. Technically, Cowboy Point was a part of Marietta.

Sometimes Knox felt like Montana was a small town all its own, despite its size. Sometimes that felt claustrophobic. Other times it felt the way it did today, like little markers wherever he looked that he was always home.

He found himself rubbing at his chest, because it was funny how much like home any and every part of Montana felt when Ramona was sitting beside him in his truck, playing him the music she liked and even singing along.

Alarm bells should have been ringing in him at that, but it was all strangely quiet.

Almost… peaceful, he might have said, when that had never been their thing. They were either making up or breaking up, and in between they'd been in bed. He had nothing to compare this to—but he liked it.

Maybe this vulnerability thing was the right move after all, no matter how unsteady it had made him feel.

But there were other things to focus on once they were in Billings.

The address that the girl in Devil's Gorge had given him led them into a fairly sad sort of neighborhood where all the houses looked on the rundown side of weathered. There were broken-down vehicles in the yards, covered with snow—but not enough to hide the state most of them were in. He found the house he was looking for and pulled up in front.

Then sat there.

Beside him, Ramona reached over and put her hand on his leg. "Are you ready?" she asked, and on this side of last night's revelations and vulnerabilities, that calm tone of hers was soothing. "It's okay if you're not. We don't have to do this at all and we certainly don't have to do it now."

Knox found that his chest was even tighter now. All he could think of was Hailey. The little noises she made. The way she kicked her feet. The sweet, solid weight of her against his chest. The way she looked when she was sleeping, so hard and deep he sometimes checked her to see if she was breathing.

"I think you and I agree that Shoshana is probably in one kind of trouble or another," Knox said after a moment, his eyes on the little house though he was still thinking about Hailey. About her cold cheeks and the wailing sound she'd made on his porch—and what if she hadn't? He didn't like to think about that. So he thought about it all the time. He had to focus to think about Shoshana Delaney now, the reason he was here in Billings. "And she chose me to help with some of the trouble she's in, so what the hell. Let's help her with all of it."

When he glanced beside him, Ramona was smiling at him. And her eyes were so soft that it was like he could feel them inside of him. Turning him inside out whether he liked it or not.

"I think that's an excellent plan," she said with a nod, and Knox would have come and done this on his own. He knew that. It was the right thing to do. It was about Hailey, not his feelings about what had been done to her—or what could have happened to her.

But it all settled on him better that Ramona was here, and that she thought he was doing the right thing. He wasn't sure when her opinion had started mattering so much to him.

Maybe around the time she'd become his first call.

Knox had to order himself to keep his head in the game. When he got out of the truck, she met him at the curb. It was cold, with a sharp wind that made it worse, but they stood there for a moment anyway. She looked up at him and then went up on the toes of her boots and kissed him on his cheek. He leaned into it, just for a second.

Then they walked over the half-heartedly shoveled snow that made a haphazard path toward the sullen front door, all chipped paint and a distinct sense of desolation. This was not a house that anyone had tried to make cheerful. Maybe ever.

Though it was a major upgrade from Devil's Gorge, all the same.

"I'll knock," Ramona said as they got to the front step, and looked back at him for confirmation that he was okay with that.

He understood the strategy. She wanted him to keep his distance at first, in case whoever was on the other side of the door here had an issue with a big cowboy showing up uninvited on the doorstep.

A baby at the door was a lot less intimidating. He got that.

Ramona had to knock more than once, but they could both see that smoke was coming from the chimney. There was the sound of a loud television set inside, though it cut off after the third round of knocking.

And when the door opened, Knox braced himself—

But he recognized her.

The girl who had to be Shoshana Delaney looked to be about the same age as the one he'd seen in Devil's Gorge. That wasn't why he recognized her, though. She was skinnier than he remembered—much skinnier than she probably should have been after having a baby in the last two months, though what did he know. Her hair was the same coppery color as the tuft on Hailey's head, or it was where he could see it coming out from beneath the knit hat she wore.

"Oh my God," Shoshana whispered, her eyes flying wide. "Is the baby okay? How did you find me? Nothing happened to the baby, did it?"

"Hailey's fine," Knox told her. "But are you?"

Shoshana stared up at him, looking stunned, like maybe no one had asked her that question in a while. Since the last time he'd asked her that question, maybe. She was wearing a

T-shirt with a cartoon character on the front. Her jeans were ripped in a way that suggested use, not fashion. She had tattoos on her hands that looked like she'd drawn them by hand, more earrings than ears, and too much eye makeup.

She didn't look old enough to be anyone's mother, though he knew that wasn't how the world worked.

He shook his head. "I know you."

"I'm so sorry." Shoshana's eyes filled with tears. "You were so kind to me and I didn't know what else to do."

Ramona moved closer, then, and put a hand on the girl's arm. Knox didn't know how she managed to do that so smoothly. Because she made it seem so unthreatening, so *warm*, when Shoshana Delaney looked like the very definition of twitchy.

"Why don't we go inside?" Ramona suggested. "We can talk. Maybe where it's a little bit warmer?"

Shoshana looked startled. She wiped at her face, and her fingers came away smudged with black. She glanced over her shoulder, like she couldn't remember what state the room was in.

"Yeah," she said after a moment. "I mean, it's okay, but not for too long. I'm not supposed to have visitors."

She turned and walked inside and they followed, exchanging glances as they went.

Inside the house, it was almost overwhelmingly hot thanks to a woodstove in one corner. It smelled of old, fried food. And it looked very much the way Knox expected. If the shacks in Devil's Gorge had electricity and stained industrial carpets, they'd pretty much be this.

But it was still an upgrade. He hoped it really was. For her sake.

Shoshana went and sat on an exhausted-looking sofa in the middle of the room, curling her knees up beneath her. Knox thought she looked like a baby herself.

"How did you find me?" Shoshana asked. Her movements were a little jerky, but Knox thought that was adrenaline, not more dangerous substances. And that was something. "I didn't tell anyone I was coming here. I needed to get away from my family for a while, that's all, and my friend said I could stay here a while." She looked from Knox to Ramona, then back again. "I didn't think you knew who I was."

"You didn't just put my name on the birth certificate," Knox reminded her. "You put yours, too."

"Oh yeah," she said, and sighed. "You have to."

Knox looked over at Ramona, who was back in unreadable mode, but her gaze was fixed on the girl sitting before them. She had also sat down on the couch, and somehow managed to look as if she had never been more at ease in her life. She exuded *everything is going to be fine* like it was a perfume. No wonder she was already everyone's favorite doctor.

And his favorite everything else, but that was going to have to wait.

He focused on the matter at hand. "I didn't know your name until I saw it on the birth certificate," he told Shoshana. "And I'm going to need you to walk me through how we went from me giving you a ride home from a questionable situation outside the Wolf Den in Marietta to you pretending that I'm the father of your baby on a birth certificate."

Ramona shifted slightly at that, like she'd wanted those details more than he'd thought she did, but Knox kept looking at Shoshana.

The girl rubbed her palms over her face. "I just…"

She didn't say anything for a moment. Knox wasn't sure she would. He was standing by the television, and he leaned forward, thinking he would ask the question a different way, maybe. But Ramona shook her head.

Wait, she mouthed.

Knox waited. And when Shoshana took her hands away, there were tears trickling down the side of her face in dark, black rivulets.

"That was a rough situation," she agreed, her voice choked. But she kept going. "I shouldn't have… That's the thing about Johnny. You think he's changed, but he never really does. Anyway, I shouldn't have been there." She focused on Knox, and swiped at the water on her face. "The thing is, you were the first man who was ever kind to me. Without asking for something. You know?"

Knox thought that the way she said that, so matter-of-factly and with such a wealth of hard-won, bitter experience in her voice, might have broken his heart all over again.

"I'm honored," he told her, and he meant that. "And I don't know what kind of situation you're in now, but I'm guessing it isn't great because you left Hailey with me."

On a cold porch outside, but he didn't need to remind either one of that. He figured that if it haunted him, it probably haunted her too.

He took a deep breath and pushed on, because there was something he needed to say to her and he didn't want to say it. It actually *hurt* that he had to.

"If you want to keep your baby, Shoshana, I will help you do that," he told her, and it took everything he had not just to say it, but to keep his voice steady. Even. He was pretty sure that Ramona's eyes were welling up too. He kept his on Shoshana. "You don't have to give her up if that's not really what you want. I don't know if leaving her was your choice, or someone made you, or—"

"No, no," the girl said at once, shaking her head. She even held her hands up, as if to ward off the very idea. "I can't have a baby. I can't… She deserves better than all this."

"So do you," Knox told her gently.

Shoshana's eyes filled, and she placed her fingers together in her lap. "That's a very kind thing to say. You're very kind. I know it's not fair, what I did. But I kept thinking that she was just this innocent baby. That she was going to come out and end up like this, and I just couldn't…" She shook her head again, dashing her hands across her eyes. "I want her to have a better life. And I know that you can give her that. Me?" She let out a hollow laugh. "They called me a lost cause in middle school. Maybe they were right, but I figured if I could do *one* good thing…"

She didn't finish that. She looked away. And Knox, for the second time in two days, wanted to bodily remove a teenager from her situation—but the same rules applied today as they had yesterday. He couldn't. Kidnapping was kidnapping no matter who was doing it. No matter what the reasons were.

"You must think I'm a terrible person," Shoshana said in a broken sort of voice. "I know I would."

She snuck a look at Ramona, who shook her head. "I don't think anything of the kind," she assured the girl. "You don't seem like a terrible person to me at all. You seem like a mother who's had to make one of the hardest choices possible."

"I think you're incredibly brave," Knox added. He had no experience with teenagers. Just like he had no experience with babies. So he thought about the things his father had said to him when he was young and filled with too many feelings he couldn't sort out. "There is no shame in admitting that things are hard and that you can't do them. That's not shameful at all. It's real strength, Shoshana. Asking for help takes courage. You should be proud of yourself."

Something about that rang in him, maybe a little too hard.

But Shoshana was swallowing hard, then she nodded. "What do you want me to do? Do I need to sign something? Because I will. I'll sign anything."

This had been part of what he'd discussed with Atticus the night before. What happened if he did find this girl. What the options were. Why it was maybe a good thing that she'd put him on the birth certificate, because it gave him standing to act in the child's interest. Atticus had given him a little primer on birth certificate fraud, and more than that, paternity rights and parental rights in general. Enough to know what he needed to do here.

"I'll make you a deal," he said to Shoshana, very seriously. "You gave me responsibility for Hailey, and I accept that responsibility. If you sign away your parental rights, I won't take you to court for committing fraud."

The girl's eyes went wide. "Fraud? What do you mean?"

"You can't just write random names on a birth certificate," he told her, but he smiled. "I'm not mad. I don't want to take you to court. You seem pretty sure that you don't want Hailey. I want to make sure of that because I don't want to take her from you." She started to lift her hands again, so he kept going. "If I do take her, I want to make sure she's mine, no matter what. Do you understand?"

Shoshana blew out a breath. "Sure," she said after a moment. "You want to make sure that I don't show up a few years from now and snatch her back from the only home she's ever known. See? I knew I picked the right guy."

But there was something so cynical about that, as if Shoshana could already see herself in that role. As if she knew that she could never be anything but a liability in her baby's life. Knox couldn't say he liked it.

"Okay," Knox said, and he held out his hand so they could shake on it. "Whatever happens, we're agreed on this. No one pushed anyone into anything."

Again, Shoshana looked a little too old for her age. "Aside from me forcing you into this, you mean."

He grinned at her. "I can take it."

And slowly, solemnly, Shoshana shook his hand.

Knox knew, somehow, that she meant it. She wasn't going to go back on this decision. And that meant that Hailey was his. Entirely his. Unless and until he came up with a better plan.

But something inside of him seemed to shift a little too precipitously at that thought.

He pushed that aside. "But there's more to this deal," he told Shoshana.

He looked at Ramona, and while he wouldn't call the expression on her face *unreadable* in the usual sense, he couldn't say he knew what it was, either. Just that it made him feel even more stripped bare than he had in the kitchen, right before he stood up.

Like this was all one vulnerability on top of the next when he'd never been one to admit he had any. He told himself this had to be good for him.

Knox focused on the girl. "This isn't the kind of deal where we never see each other again, Shoshana. You can always come to me for help. You already know where I live."

She looked abashed at that. "After that thing at the Wolf Den, when you took me to my uncle's place in Marietta, I followed you home. I just wanted to see what it looked like in your world. I didn't mean any harm. I didn't even know I was pregnant then."

He smiled. "I don't mind. I'm glad you found a safe place for Hailey."

All he could think of was Shoshana hiding in the trees, peering at his house. He remembered where he'd dropped her off in Marietta, a tidy little house with a fifth wheel parked beside it. He'd waited until she'd gone into the trailer before he'd left her there. And he'd wished he'd done more than scare off the guy who'd been giving her trouble with a *look.*

But he couldn't change the past, so he kept going. "You can come by whenever you like to see Hailey. I won't keep her from you. I just want to make sure that she always knows who she is and where she lives, and who her acting parent is. For her sake."

That's what he'd been thinking about on the drive here, when he wasn't thinking about Ramona. Assuming Shoshana wasn't wracked with guilt and remorse, assuming she didn't want Hailey back—as hard as that was for him to imagine— what sort of home did Hailey deserve?

"I get it," Shoshana said, and he didn't think he was imagining that she sounded relieved. "I knew you'd be the right choice."

He stepped away then to call the lawyer he knew in Billings, who he'd prepped yesterday while he was grabbing food. He told him what had been agreed and signed off on the next steps. Then he asked if a lawyer could be found for Shoshana, too, just to make sure that everything was above board for her. He assured his friend that he'd be the one paying no matter what the court decided about Shoshana's involvement.

While he was on the phone, Ramona sat and talked with Shoshana about options. Safe spaces. Ramona even made a few calls herself, to people she knew out this way who could offer Shoshana a different path, if she liked.

"I think I will call," Shoshana said when Ramona texted her a list of places. "I might… I don't know, I think maybe I want to get my GED after all."

Ramona nodded in that solemn, doctor-y way of hers that made it seem like Shoshana's success was a foregone conclusion. "I think that's a terrific idea."

When they got up to leave, they'd started the legal proceedings as best they could in one afternoon. Knox had Shoshana sign a letter of intent, just in case things got weird, though he didn't think they would. Ramona had inspired the girl. He'd seen it all over her face.

"You can text me anytime," Ramona told her as they walked out.

"Me too," Knox said.

Shoshana looked… almost hopeful, Knox thought. She even attempted a smile. "If you wanted to send me a picture of the baby, every now and again. Only if you feel like it. Just… you know, to see how she's doing."

"Count on it," Knox said gruffly.

On the drive back, Ramona called around to the people she knew to see if they might reach out to Shoshana or if they knew someone who could help a teenager in a precarious situation. So she wouldn't be stranded. So she really could do that GED and change the course of her life, if she wanted.

"I don't know if she'll actually want help, in the end," Ramona said, as they drove up Copper Mountain. Nice and slow, because the temperature was dropping. "But if she does, there are a bunch of people who will be happy to give it."

And when they made it back to Cowboy Point, Knox didn't even pretend that he might stop at her place. She didn't ask. Instead, he drove them back up to the ranch, and took her inside his parents' house when he went to pick up the baby.

He thought Ramona might balk at that, but she didn't. She walked in at his side as if it was the most normal, everyday thing in the world. As if it wasn't even worthy of comment, that's how much they belonged together.

And he waited for those alarms inside him to sound, the

way they always did. The way they always had, warning him that he was getting too close and giving her the wrong idea.

But there was nothing in him but that *contented* feeling again.

Cat and Sierra were in the living room with Belinda, the twin boys, and sweet little Hailey.

"We're making ourselves useful," Sierra said, looking up from an intense toy battle with Eli and Levi on the floor.

"I'm pumping this baby for information," Cat said, from where she was sitting on the couch with Belinda, Hailey lying on a blanket between them. But she was looking at Ramona, speculation bright and hot in her gaze.

"Boone and Wilder gathered all that baby stuff from everyone else," Sierra continued, with only a glance at Cat. When she looked back at Ramona and Knox, her gaze was clear. "They set it all up in your house already, so it's waiting for you when you get back."

"How thoughtful," Knox said with a laugh. He went to pick Hailey up and realized that he'd been holding his breath until then. Until he could feel the sweet weight of her, there in his arms like she belonged there. "Are you sure it was Boone and Wilder?"

That made everyone laugh.

Then he and Ramona left with the baby, and Ramona held her as they headed down the hill.

"I need to get a car seat fitted," Knox muttered. "It's not safe."

Ramona slid him a look he couldn't read, which wasn't new, but this one was bright and warm. Because he guessed upgrades were going around.

"If you take it to Atticus or the Marietta police, they can put it in for you and make sure it's done right," she told him. "They've made them so complicated these days that a lot of people need help installing them."

Knox felt certain he could figure it out, or make Harlan and Ryder show him, but he didn't say that out loud. He was enjoying the fact that they were discussing Hailey like this. Like they were a unit.

It made that peaceful feeling in him expand, until it seemed like it was taking him over.

In the house, there were diapers and bottling systems, and other baby things he wasn't sure he could identify, stacked up in the kitchen. Back down the hall, he saw that his brothers had taken over the guest room closest to Knox's room and made it Hailey's. And they'd done it up. There wasn't just a crib, there was also a mobile hanging from the ceiling, with little lambs in a circle. And there were tiny clothes that were all hand-me-down boys' stuff, a playpen, and other items he'd never heard of that looked adorable and off-putting at once.

Hailey was sleepy, even though it was early, so Knox put her down in her new crib and sang to her. A tuneless little song that was more of a memory. Belinda had sung it to him when he was little. She'd probably sung it to him over his crib, just like this.

After a little bit of perfunctory fussing, Hailey went to sleep, and Knox walked back out into the great room.

Ramona was waiting for him, but she wasn't lounging on the couch. She'd started going through the things his brothers had left, and pointed at the cartons of formula they'd left him. Correctly anticipating that he would need it to feed Hailey—though he had enough to get them through to tomorrow, thanks to his mother.

One more thing he was going to have to get on top of.

Ramona stopped organizing things and came over to him, walking right into him and wrapping her arms around his waist. Then she snuggled in and hugged him.

"You," she said, tipping her head back to look up at him, "are a remarkable man."

The hug felt good. This all felt good. He liked that she was here. It felt right, like he'd told her. But it was more than that.

They still fit.

Like they were made for each other.

Even with all their clothes on. It wasn't that he didn't want her, because he couldn't imagine a scenario where he wouldn't want her, but it wasn't driving him just now. This was simply… a hug. Leaning into each other. Peace and comfort and a different sort of warmth that seemed to come from the inside of him.

He wasn't sure he'd ever hugged anyone like this, unless

maybe it was Belinda, long ago. But his older brothers had teased him for wanting to be cuddled, so he'd decided he didn't like it anymore when he was in kindergarten.

Now he was wondering why he'd listened to those idiots.

Knox held her close, and it felt like all of his boundaries and rules and alarms were just... melting away. He put his chin on the top of her head. He breathed her in.

He thought that he was going to have to find a way to make this go on forever.

Ramona melted into him. She let out a sigh, and then she smiled at him a little dreamily. "I love you," she said.

And he froze. It was involuntary. He heard the words and he reacted.

He went stiff, head to toe, like that alarm he'd been so surprised not to hear was ringing at last. But then it didn't matter what was happening inside of him, because Ramona was pushing away from him.

"Hey," he said. "I didn't—"

She lifted a hand, and he stopped talking. For a moment it was like she was studying him, and there was something about the way she did it that made everything in him run cold.

"I should have known better," she said.

Softly. Quietly.

Devastatingly.

"Ramona—"

"I told myself that it didn't matter what we called this, or what you said you did or didn't feel, but I was lying to myself," she told him, and what was different was that she didn't look mad. She didn't look upset.

She looked something like *resigned*, and it made him want to claw back these past few minutes and do them over. And better.

"It was just a knee-jerk reaction," he told her.

"I'm sure it was. But you can make it up to me, right? It's simple." Now she folded her arms in front of her chest and her blue gaze got narrow. "Just say it back."

"What?"

"You heard me."

"Ramona, this isn't what—"

"Say it," she said again, and he understood, then, that she wasn't mad or upset.

She was furious. Coldly, intensely furious.

He opened his mouth, but nothing came out. He tried again, but it was like he was caught in the grip of a tight, hard fist and he had no idea how to loosen it.

"Perfect," Ramona breathed, and he could see a new kind of light in her gaze. It was not even remotely warm. "I can't even blame you. You've repeatedly told me and showed me who you are. I'm the one who keeps pretending you might magically turn into someone else."

"I've never cared about anyone the way I care about you," he managed to get out, though it felt like knives in his throat.

"Do you really?" She stepped forward then, and poked a finger into his chest. "I think you're full of shit."

"I am a lot of things, I grant you," he began, but she poked him again. Harder.

"You're wildly, madly, unbearably in love with me, you idiot," she threw at him. "You have been since the night we met, the same as me. And you're never leaving Cowboy Point. You love it here. Your family means everything to you. Sometimes I think the only reason you even talk about leaving is because you told your brothers you would, and now you refuse to back down."

He thought maybe his mouth dropped open, but he couldn't seem to find any words.

Ramona had no such problem. "I don't know why I thought that everything changed. That Hailey changed you. That the fact you've decided to keep her means that you—"

"I haven't decided anything," he argued, a kind of panic gripping him by the throat.

That made Ramona rock back on her heels. She looked at him as if she'd never seen him before. "You can't be serious. You're head over heels in love with that baby. Do you really think you're going to hand her off to someone else? Are you truly that delusional?"

Knox didn't know what he was, but it felt like an earthquake. Maybe a series of earthquakes and a volcanic eruption for good measure.

"Ramona," he tried again, but she was turning and walking away from him.

She went over to the door and stamped her feet into her boots.

"That's fine," she told him. "Stay right here in your mausoleum of a house and pretend that your life is going to start someday soon. In the meantime, definitely don't admit to yourself that you already have a better life than most." She glared at him as she jerked her sweater on over her head and jammed her arms into the sleeves of her coat. "That baby already adores you. Your family dotes on you. And you and I have something pretty special, but you're too busy imagining far-off horizons to pay attention to where you're standing."

"Ramona."

"I'm going to get Cat or Sierra to drive me back into Cowboy Point," she told him. "I'm not staying here, and that sucks, Knox, because I like staying here. I like everything that's happened between us since Christmas Eve, and I'm just sorry that none of that seemed to reach you."

"Ramona, I don't want to lose you," he gritted out, like it was torn out of him.

"Lose me?" She shook her head at him, her eyes dark. "You would have to actually *be in this* for five seconds to lose it. You would have to *choose me*. You would have to actually let yourself love something without walling yourself off from how it feels. You don't lose anything when I walk out this door." Ramona's gaze seemed to spear straight through him. "You never let yourself have me, did you?"

She didn't wait for an answer. Maybe she knew that no answers were forthcoming. She merely turned, opened the door, and walked outside. Then she shut it behind her—quietly.

That was even worse.

And it left him feeling like he'd been struck down by some kind of giant stone that had landed hard and was pressing and pressing—

Knox shook it off, somehow, and he staggered to the door. He threw himself out into the cold and went to the edge of the porch in his socks, the cold seeping into him, so frigid it felt like a burn.

But she was gone.

And this time he knew that there was no possible way that she was ever coming back.

Chapter Ten

NEW YEAR'S EVE had never been a favorite holiday for Ramona. She'd either been working, and therefore getting a close-up view of the excesses involved, or she'd been happily sequestering herself away from the world.

This year she could do neither.

Cat had been only too happy to pick her up the day before. She must have come running out of the ranch house the moment Ramona's text hit her phone because she managed to get down the hill in record time, snow be damned. Ramona had barely made it out to the main drive when Cat pulled up in an oversized truck.

I take it things got less cozy than they looked a little while ago, Cat said when Ramona slammed her way into the passenger seat, cold from the walk down Knox's drive but making up for it with temper.

She put her seat belt on with perhaps too much aggression.

Things came to their inevitable conclusion, she said. *The way they always do. Maybe this time I'll learn something.*

Ouch, Cat had replied. And Ramona must have sounded a little more bitter than she usually did, because Cat didn't follow that up with more questions.

She had spoken with Cat a million times about Knox. Her friend knew more than she probably should have about her own brother-in-law. It would have been the easiest thing in the world to download on her all over again now. Cat had certainly made it clear, time and again, that she was willing to listen.

But something in Ramona just wouldn't let her do it.

I don't want to talk about him, she said instead, as they bumped their slow way down the hill and out beneath the High Mountain Ranch gates. *I have a date with Wyatt Stark to that New Year's party at the Lodge tomorrow night. That's what I'm going to focus on. The future.*

Sure, Cat murmured, much too agreeably. *You know what they say. Best way to get over one man—*

Ramona had shot her a look. Cat had gone quiet.

The fact was, Ramona thought now as she closed up the clinic late on the afternoon of December 31, she had completely forgotten that she had a date with Wyatt Stark. She had completely forgotten about the existence of the man, along with pretty much everything else that wasn't Knox or Hailey. It had come back to her as she'd been regretting her urge to storm off from Knox's house.

She hadn't regretted leaving. She had regretted that it was a harder walk than it should have been because of the snow piled high all around. It was all packed down into twin grooves by the truck wheels that had run over it, but it still wasn't quite as smooth a walk as she might have liked.

Ramona had stomped along and it was almost like she'd suffered too huge a loss to be able to look at it directly. It was too all-encompassing. There were too many implications to face head-on out there on a cold afternoon, the December light eking away toward the west when it had barely had time to establish itself.

It had been easier to focus on the way he had flinched when she'd told him she loved him.

What was there to say about that? It spoke for itself. It spoke loudly. It was more of a shout, really.

She hadn't cried. She hadn't shouted. What was the point? She had done all of that so many times and she'd still ended up right back there in the same place.

She'd also realized while stomping around out there in the cold that she'd kind of forgotten what day it was. Maybe that was a good thing. Maybe the fact that it was New Year's Eve the following night could make everything right, she had thought. She could turn the page. It would be a new year and she knew that she would start that year on a date with a man who had already proven himself to be good company. Wyatt was easy to talk to. Ramona found him entertaining. He was undeniably good-looking.

The only thing she had ever not liked about him was that he wasn't Knox.

Even thinking that had stiffened her resolve as she'd clambered through the woods.

The Starks in Wyatt's generation had been redoing their family's showpiece lodge for years now. They intended to open the main lodge in the next summer or so. In the meantime, they had renovated the smaller cottages and outbuildings that stood around the Lodge proper and trickled down the hill toward Cowboy Point's main road. They had taken in their first guests in the cottages this fall, and had also rented the cottages closer to the Lodge to local business owners, like Rosie. To celebrate all of these steps forward after a generation of disrepair before them, they were throwing a big New Year's Eve bash.

There were fancy parties down in Marietta, like in the beautiful Graff Hotel, but this would be the first time that there was a destination requiring a nice dress on this side of Copper Mountain.

On the upside, Wyatt had told her with a grin, if the weather turned bad they had a lot of places for people to stay—even if it was still a little more like camping in some parts of the old lodge.

Ramona locked the door to the clinic behind her and headed up the inside stairs to her apartment. Her head had been so full of baby Hailey and Knox and going to Billings to find Shoshana, that it had taken her a solid hour or two to decompress once she'd finally gotten home yesterday. She'd taken a long bath. She'd tried to cry it out, but no tears had come.

Slowly, slowly she had started breathing again.

The real problem with all of this, she acknowledged now as she moved through her apartment and stripped off her work clothes to get in the shower, was that his being a jackass didn't change the fact that she was in love with him.

Nothing seemed to change that.

She knew too much about him, though. She had her theories about why he was the way he was—not that it ever seemed to help her any since he didn't want to face himself.

It didn't matter what she thought. It mattered what he did.

And once again, he'd done the same thing he always did.

If she wanted to change things, she was going to have to do it herself. By herself.

"It's okay," she told herself as she got out of the shower tonight and wrapped herself up in her warm, soft towel. "Everyone backslides now and again. It's all about starting over. Again."

Though she could feel how different it was this time, deep in her bones. No sobbing—so intensely that sometimes she'd thought she might throw up. No raging into her pillows, punching them all so hard that one time she'd actually made feathers fly up all around her.

It came to her while she was getting dressed that all of the times she'd grieved him before, some part of her had still held on to hope.

But it was the person who lived who grieved, she thought as she zipped up her dress. This felt like a death.

Wyatt had offered to pick her up, but Ramona had insisted that she would drive herself. It was a particular Montana kind of fancy, she thought, to dress up pretty and do her hair and makeup *just so*. And then wrap herself up in a huge coat, a hat that would likely wreck her hair, and have to carry her shoes because she needed boots to get out to her truck.

She drove herself through Cowboy Point, and blew out a long sort of breath as she did. It was still so pretty here. That was something she kept coming back to, every time her heart broke.

It was tempting to think that she could pick up and move somewhere else, then get over Knox by virtue of geography. But she figured that then she would be just as sad and also somewhere that wasn't here, which seemed like punishment.

This had always been her favorite place in the world.

Ramona didn't see why Knox's continuing emotional constipation should take Cowboy Point away from her too. This was her home now, no matter what he did or didn't do.

The tiny little town looked pretty on the last night of the year. Everything was closed, but all of the shop owners had put up lights and made it festive. The main street sparkled there against the wild Montana dark. There were lights up on the surrounding ridges, little outposts against the presence of the towering mountains.

At the top of the ridge across from her driveway was Dallas Lisle's lighthouse, and he had the light beaming around tonight, sweeping this way and that. She liked it. And was looking forward to the bed-and-breakfast that the rumor was he'd be opening next fall.

Everywhere she looked, there were signs that Cowboy Point was having the kind of renaissance that would have horrified her grandfather, who would have preferred the whole community to be little more than the old mine and few outposts. He would have lived in a tent on the mountain all year-round if he could.

But things were changing. There was a new restaurant coming on the main street, though no one was quite sure who owned it or what kind of restaurant it would be yet. Boone and Sierra's artisan dairy kept getting written up in fancy publications, as did the many food trucks—more every summer, run by folks who didn't want the hassle of restaurant overheads, but wanted to share the things they made with the world. More people were moving to Cowboy Point than away, which was a big deal in remote, rural communities.

Ramona had no intention of leaving.

No matter what Knox Carey did or didn't do.

She felt that even more intently when she made it up the hill to Cowboy Point Lodge.

It looked especially pretty tonight with all its lights blazing. It stood as a kind of beacon, there on a hill across from the snow-covered peak of Copper Mountain.

Ramona parked in the big lot, pleased to see that it was packed. She made her way carefully toward the big front doors, nodding as she ran into familiar faces along the way.

Inside, the big lobby had a couple of teenage girls on hand to take all the snowy boots and coats, handing out tickets and running it like a proper coat check. Ramona had only been to an event here once before. It had been a surprise reception for Ryder and Rosie last spring, and the place had still felt largely unfinished.

Tonight it gleamed. It had been built in the Victorian style, like the many grand railway hotels that dotted the West, though it was hard to imagine anyone believed trains would venture this high in the mountains. It was supposed to open fully as a hotel again the summer after next, but Ramona liked that the Starks kept reminding Cowboy Point that it had once been at the heart of the community here.

There was a band in the old ballroom. People were dancing, but Ramona wasn't a dancer. She moved around the edge of the ballroom, then walked across the hall into another grand room, where food had been laid out on tables draped in glittering fabrics and decorated with candelabras that looked like they belonged in a Gothic romance. There was a bar on the other end of the room, and high tables in between for people to cluster around, having drinks and looking entirely unlike themselves.

There were a lot of suit coats and cowboy hats on men she normally associated with plaid shirts and Wranglers. But then, Ramona was usually in her scrubs and white coat at the clinic, so she wasn't one to talk. Tonight she'd gone for the sort of gown she never got to wear here. It had a high neck, but no arms and no back. It flowed in gleaming royal blue all the way down to the ground. She also wore a little bit of sparkle at her ears and had piled her hair up on top of her head into something that nodded toward elegant.

She thought she'd cleaned up all right.

And when Wyatt Stark came toward her, grinning, she figured she'd hit the right note.

"You made it," he said, in that low drawl of his that Ramona dearly wished she found as effective as it should have been.

He had the dark hair, gray eyes, and stern mouth of all the Stark boys. Ramona had learned that when people used the term *Stark boys*, it meant not only Wyatt, his two brothers, and their cousin Jack, but all of the Stark men who had come before them. Meaning their fathers, living and dead. Maybe their grandfather too.

She knew that Wyatt and his brothers were considered wild and disreputable, but she figured that was mostly because they were all excessively good-looking, and very single.

Ramona didn't say any of that. She only smiled. "I made it," she agreed.

He got her a drink and she took it. They stood together at one of the high-top tables, and it was nice. Really, Ramona thought, it was *so nice*. They talked about nice things. He was interested in what she had to say, he made her laugh, and he was a terrific date. She knew that already.

She should have been having a fantastic time, but instead, she thought that she'd never felt quite so sad and alone in all her life. It was unfair to her date, so she smiled. She laughed.

Maybe if she pretended she was fine, she would be. Eventually.

The music changed in the ballroom. More people came inside. The party got louder, jollier. And then she felt a prickle at the back of her neck.

When she turned, Knox was there.

He was dressed in the Cowboy Point uniform tonight. A black suit that fit him beautifully, and a dressy black Stetson to go with it. She knew that if she looked down at his feet, he would be wearing one of his good pairs of cowboy boots. The kind a man never wore out on the range, but only out on the town.

His eyes found hers immediately, looking dark and coppery tonight. It was like there was a tractor beam connecting them, and nothing made sense until it snapped into place.

And even though Ramona knew better, her heart leaped in her chest. She felt immediately lighter. Better.

Damn that man.

"Ramona," Wyatt said from beside her. She turned back to him, hoping her face hadn't betrayed her. But Wyatt was looking across the room, over toward Knox. "I don't mean to dig too far into your personal business, but I'm guessing that your heart's not really in this."

When he turned to look at her again, she got a glimpse of exactly who Wyatt Stark would be for the right woman. Devastating. Calmly authoritative, but in this moment, something like amused.

"I'm sorry," she told him. "I didn't mean to get distracted."

"You don't look at me the way you look at Knox Carey," Wyatt said simply. "And between you and me, Knox doesn't look at anyone the way he looks at you."

He tipped his hat, and Ramona felt terrible.

"I'm so sorry," she said. "I didn't mean—"

"You don't owe me any apologies," he assured her. "This is our fourth date and you haven't even let me pick you up. Much less kiss you. I was beginning to think I'd lost my touch." His mouth curved. "My ego is happy to discover that it's just that you've already got a claim on your heart."

Ramona wanted to argue about that, but she was too aware of Knox across the room.

"Happy New Year," Wyatt murmured, and then walked away.

She wanted to beg him to stay. She wanted to make wild promises she didn't mean. She wanted to argue with him because what she *really* didn't want was to deal with Knox, who was now stalking toward her as if he didn't realize that there were other people in this room.

He drew close and she shook her head at him. "We have nothing to say to each other," she told him.

"I feel certain that you have nothing to say to me, Ramona, and that's okay," Knox replied. "It turns out, I have a thing or two to say to you." But he didn't launch into any speeches. He held out his hand instead. "You've never danced with me."

She made a face. "That's because I hate dancing."

"*That's* because you've never danced with me," he retorted.

He didn't take her hand himself, though he could have. He waited.

And Ramona hated this. She needed to be done with him. That had been absolutely clear to her yesterday. There could be no backsliding again—she wasn't sure she'd survive it.

Then again, he'd come here tonight. He'd sought her out, and not in the dark of night. She'd spent a lot of time thinking about that yesterday. She'd curled up in the fetal position on her couch and she'd wondered why it had never really dawned on her that everything they did they did alone. Isolated. Usually at night, and then snuck away by morning.

He'd never taken her on a date. He'd never taken her anywhere, except to Billings.

But another thing he'd never done was walk up to her in a crowded room and then stand there, his hand outstretched.

She knew that people were watching. She could even hear a few whispers.

Knox didn't say another word. He just kept that gaze of his locked to hers, and his hand hanging in the air between them.

"Fine," Ramona said, crossly.

She pretended it was because she didn't want to be stared at anymore. She pretended that this was simply the *expedient* way out of this situation, and she slid her hand into his.

They were staring at each other, so she knew she wasn't the only one to feel that immediate spark between them when they touched, and then to see the answering flare of it in his gaze the way she knew it was in hers.

There was nothing *expedient* about touching Knox.

He held her hand for a moment, like he was winded, but to Ramona it seemed like a lifetime.

It had to be at least a lifetime and several eternities later when he turned and tugged her with him as he wound his way through their friends and neighbors, stopping for none of them, and took her out onto the dance floor.

He was right, they had never danced together. If they had, she would have known better than to agree to it now.

Because he pulled her into his arms, and this wasn't some historical drama. He didn't break out in a waltz.

He put his arms around her, his hands on the naked skin of her back. And she lifted her arms so she could put her hands on his shoulders, which meant she was pressed against him.

And it suddenly struck her as outrageous that people were allowed to do this in public.

She braced herself as they swayed back and forth, while one of the old-timers who hung out at the General Store most days did a surprisingly good Frank Sinatra impression at the mic.

There were no speeches from Knox. No inadequate discussions of how much he *cared* about her.

They just danced. One song, then the next.

Ramona wondered if he was doing this deliberately. If he knew that the more he touched her, the more she would find herself helpless to refuse him anything.

Try a spine on for size, she snapped at herself, the way her grandfather had—though he'd done it with a twinkle in his eye. Ramona did not feel *twinkly.*

After the third song, he led her off the dance floor. She thought that he was going to head back into the other room with the bar and the food, but instead he ducked down a smaller hall that led away from the party.

"Where are you going?" she asked.

"Trust me," he replied.

She wanted to tell him that was the last thing she was likely to do, but she didn't. Because as strange as it seemed, she did trust him. Maybe not to take good care of her heart, but with everything else.

With that baby, for one thing. It hadn't once occurred to her to call social services because she'd known he had it covered. With his family. With his friends. With all the parts of the life he didn't think he wanted, and yet had arranged around himself just the same.

He led her up a flight of stairs that looked very different from the grand set of stairs that swept down from the second-floor landing of the Lodge and ended, splendidly, in the lobby. But when they arrived at the top, she saw they were up at the top of those grand stairs anyway.

"There's a back way?" she asked with a laugh. "What are those, the servants' stairs?"

"Exactly," Knox supplied.

And on this side of the landing, they weren't within sight of anyone below. Instead, they were closer to the huge window that was the focal point of the stairs and the lobby, rising high above both.

The window looked out over Cowboy Point, over to Copper Mountain, and beyond. The smudge in the distance, that string of light, had to be Marietta. Ramona could see the whole of her little community, but from a different perspective than she usually had when she was driving up and down the same roads far below.

It looked magical. Enchanted, even.

And when she looked back at Knox, he was watching her as if he found her both of those things.

Her heart seemed to skip a beat.

"I love you," he said then, fiercely.

And her breath left her body entirely.

"I have a lot of other things to say, Ramona, but I figured I'd start there," Knox continued in that same darkly determined way. "Because I want to make sure that you hear me. I love you. You're absolutely right—I think I've been in love with you since the moment I saw you sitting at that table in the pizza place. I've just been trying to run away from that ever since."

And it turned out that when he finally said the very thing that she had been wanting him to say for all of these months—since the moment she'd met him, even—she didn't have the slightest idea how to respond.

She stared back at him and she couldn't tell if she was flushed bright red or gone pale as a ghost.

Maybe both.

And then, at the worst possible moment, *that* was when her body decided that it was the perfect time to give in to all the emotions stampeding around inside of her—and cry.

Chapter Eleven

KNOX SWEPT A glance over her, taking it all in, and nodded. Of course he'd finally said the thing and she was crying. Maybe some men would take that as a slap. He couldn't see it that way, but even if it was one, he had it coming.

Though he was going to have to come to terms with how little he wanted to see Ramona cry, for any reason.

He hated it, in fact.

"I can see that you really didn't think I was going to come back," he said after a moment. "And that's pretty shitty. Of me. I hate that I make you feel this way, Ramona. But we'll circle back around on that."

He led her closer to the window and then sat her down on the little banquette that ran along the bottom of the great Lodge window like a cozier version of a windowsill.

Knox didn't join her there. He stood in front of her, staring down at her like he could share all the things that he wanted to say with the force of his mind. He wished he could.

But if he could do something like that, they wouldn't have come to this point. So he was going to have to suck it up and talk instead.

"Let's hit on a few housekeeping details first," he said, rocking back on his heels. "My parents decided to throw their own New Year's party, but only for the grandchildren. I think everyone else came here, except Ryder and Rosie, who jumped at the chance to sleep. They don't expect to be without the girls all night."

Ramona swallowed visibly, then dabbed at her damp face with her knuckles. She did not look at him. "I would think not. They're too young."

"They bunked down in one of the rooms in the ranch house, so they can have the best of both worlds. Some peaceful sleep, and access to the girls when they cry." He nodded, like he'd crossed that off the list. "But while I was there with Hailey, they all kept asking me what I'd decided." He tilted his head a little to one side. "Did you tell someone that I hadn't made up my mind yet about keeping her?"

Ramona looked at him and frowned, but only a little. "I didn't say that. I said you were appropriately considering all your options."

"There aren't any options," he told her, gruffly. He reached up and knocked his hat off his head, and then raked his hand through his hair. He set the Stetson down on the banquette beside her, then he straightened again. "After you left, I had a lot of thinking to do."

"Is that a new experience for you?"

Knox nodded, then ran his tongue around his teeth. "I

deserve that. I ran out after you, but you were already gone. And I'm not sure that would have stopped me, but what I was clear on was that you didn't want me following you. So I went back inside."

He looked past her, out toward Cowboy Point, at this view that he didn't have to know anything about real estate to know was spectacular. The kind of view that people would kill for, because it wasn't simply beautiful, it was evocative. Dallas Lisle's ridiculous lighthouse, which should have been an eyesore, instead bathed the town in light at intervals, illuminating it in swathes so it was like Knox was staring straight down into his own history as it flashed by.

The entire life he'd lived in and around this little valley hidden behind Copper Mountain.

This place he'd considered too small, too remote, and had always planned to leave.

And yet somehow, tonight, it seemed like the whole world.

Knox knew that was because Ramona was sitting here in front of him, framed by that view, the center of the universe for all intents and purposes.

The center of *him*, now that he allowed himself to accept it.

He blew out a breath. "I'm going to take you through this step by step, because I know you won't believe me if I just tell you where I ended up. Because I've given you no reason to believe me. I know that too."

She looked stunning. He had never known her *not* to look stunning, of course, but it was on a different level tonight. Every time she wore blue it was like she was turning the dimmer up. She was going from the quiet inevitability of her innate, elegant beauty straight off into the stratosphere.

He'd seen very clearly that Wyatt Stark certainly appreciated her. Not that he was jealous. He actually, truly wasn't. He knew what he and Ramona had between them hadn't disappeared overnight, and, probably, Wyatt didn't have a chance with her.

What he'd been worried about was that she would choose Wyatt anyway, because she was sick of Knox's shit.

Which would have been perfectly fair. Reasonable, even.

But she was sitting here now, looking at him. Her tears had dried, but he wouldn't say that the expression on her face was all that welcoming. It seemed a lot more like she was just waiting to see what he would say.

He reminded himself that she was a doctor. She liked data. She liked research, facts, and the compilation of supporting evidence.

Knox cleared his throat. "When Hailey woke up, I changed her and fed her. And as I was feeding her, she was staring up, and I had this wild, almost lightheaded sensation." He was holding one of his hands flexed open over his chest, but he didn't drop it when he realized he was doing it. "I was thinking about all the things you'd said to me, and I was looking at her, and it was almost as if the horizons just…"

He shook his head. "I don't know if this makes sense. But it was like I thought the world was one size. And then the more I looked at Hailey, the more I realized it was infinite, and she was the reason why, and it was obvious to me in that moment that I was only ever pretending that I was going to let someone else raise her."

Ramona pulled in a breath. Her hands were in her lap and she was holding them tight together, and Knox couldn't tell if that was because she wanted to jump up and run away, or maybe just jump up and run.

"I've never spent a single second of my life wondering what it would be like to be a father," Knox told her. "Not that I don't want a family, or didn't assume that I might someday, but I thought *someday* was far away. I had a solid idea of all the things I needed to accomplish between this day and *someday*. But the more I look at Hailey, the less I think any of that matters."

He found her gaze and held it. "I'm not giving her up. Ever. I'm not surprised that you knew that before me, but I want you to know that I know it now."

There were all kinds of things swimming around in all of the blue in her eyes, but all she did was nod. "Good," she said, quietly. Calmly. "I'm glad to hear that. And for the record, I think you'll be an excellent father."

Knox thought that sounded… not terrible, so he pushed on. "And once I realized that none of those things I thought were important mattered to me, not anymore, it was like I could finally see the past year and a half for what it was." He held her gaze. "I hope you know that I truly never meant to hurt you. I truly believed that what I was doing was protecting you, and I'm sorry that I didn't see how obviously that wasn't the case."

Her eyes closed, like they were too heavy to keep open, then she shook her head. "These are all things I've wanted to hear from you for a long time, Knox. But what's the point of it all now?"

She looked past him to where the party was carrying on below them. The music swelled. There was laughter and conversation and the clinking of glasses. It all sounded so happy, so bright.

"I thought you might say that," Knox said.

And it was a funny thing to know exactly what was supposed to happen. To finally be completely and utterly clear on what his life was meant to be.

To know that this woman wasn't only his heart, she was his clarity. She was the reason for everything.

He was going to have to live with that no matter what happened here.

Knox stopped stalling, went down on one knee, and knelt before her, watching her blue eyes widen. "I wanted to do this properly. I thought I needed to make a plan, go to Bozeman, and find something at least half as spectacular as you. But then I figured you would think that was bullshit too. A whole lot of smoke and mirrors when you still didn't know if you could trust me to tell the truth about what's happening between us."

He reached into his pocket and pulled out a small item he'd tucked in there. It wasn't in a pretty box. It was a dainty-looking ring made of hammered metal, twisted to form a unique shape. It almost looked like a stethoscope.

"Your father made that," Ramona said then, and her voice sounded thick.

"He did." Knox turned it over in his hand, admiring the workmanship. "He told me that when Kendall had it out in the booth at the market this summer, you picked it up every time you went by. And when I asked him about it tonight, and asked him if he'd sold it, he laughed at me. He told me that it had never been for sale. I thought that meant he'd given it away, but he hadn't." He moved the ring this way and that, letting the shiny metal catch the light, and make it bounce. "What he told me, Ramona, was that it's been yours all along."

What Zeke had actually said was that he had given up hoping that Knox would ever stop being a fool, and had spent months wondering if he would be better off melting the ring back down.

Is that a yes or no? Knox had asked, eyeing his prickly old father, who, he couldn't help but notice, looked remarkably fit for someone who should really have been at death's door. *Are you going to give it to me? Or do I have to beg?*

I think some begging would do you good, Zeke had replied.

But I'm not the audience.

Then he'd led Knox out to his workshop in the barn across the cold yard, and had found the ring. He'd given it a polish, completely unconcerned that Knox had somewhere to be.

You've always had to do everything the hard way, boy, Zeke had said while he worked. *You might be the most stubborn Carey that ever was, and that's saying something.*

You say that like you haven't met all the other Careys, Knox retorted.

Your brothers gave you a hard time, so you give yourself a harder time. Zeke hadn't even looked up. He was too busy with the ring. *In my day, I would never have let a beautiful woman like that doctor cry over me. That's the kind of woman you keep laughing, Knox. You keep her happy. Because she could do better than you with a snap of her fingers and why would you give her any reason to do that? I'm telling you, it's the only way.*

Knox shouldn't have been surprised that his father seemed to know everything about his life. Zeke had always been that way. He'd always known things he shouldn't.

He claimed he was simply observant, and maybe his children should try it on for size sometime.

The only way to what? Knox had asked.

The only way to you, Zeke had replied at once.

He'd handed over the ring, still warm from his hands. Knox closed his fingers around it, but he couldn't seem to take his eyes away from his father's.

To you, Zeke had said again. *Because you've been so busy proving yourself to everyone and everything that I think you lost track of you somewhere. As far as I can tell, the only time you seem to find yourself again is when you're with that Ramona.*

This is exactly the kind of advice that might have been useful months ago, Knox had retorted.

Would it? the old man shot right back at him. *Remind me when, exactly, in these past few months you were in a receptive mood to be told… anything?*

Dad, Knox had said quietly. *You've always made family look so easy.*

Because it is, Zeke had replied gruffly. *You just love them as loud and as hard as you can. And I promise you, the rest of it works itself out. One way or another.*

And that had fueled Knox as he finally headed off the ranch and down through the little tangle of unmarked roads until he could climb his way up the hill to the Lodge.

What fueled him now was that look of shock and something like wonder on Ramona's face.

He hadn't really believed that he would ever see that again.

"I love you," he said again now. "I've spent most of my life doing my best to be completely invulnerable. I never thought I had a choice. If I told my brothers this, they would hate themselves, but I did what I thought I had to do to defend against them and then it became who I am." He shook his head. "And then you turned up and made it clear that I had no defenses against you whatsoever."

"That's not how I remember it," she whispered.

He wanted to pull her into his arms, but he hadn't earned it. And he might not earn it tonight. Still, he was going to say what should have been said a long time ago.

"You taught me how to feel, and I pretended I couldn't. You showed me how to fall head over heels in love, and I pretended it was just physical. And for reasons that I will never understand, you kept forgiving me. You kept coming back. You kept letting me do it over and over again."

She looked as if she was about to speak then, but he shook his head. "I'm sure you want to say something self-deprecating, but Ramona, every time you came back, you showed me exactly what vulnerability looks like when it's actually strength. You showed me that there was no shame in leading with your feelings. Hell, your apartment is decorated like a feeling and it's the most comfortable place I've ever been in my life."

He leaned a little closer and when he couldn't hold back anymore, he put his free hand on one of her knees.

And his heart kicked into double time when she put her own hands on top of it, and held it there.

Knox kept going. "I didn't realize it soon enough, but I realize now. This whole time you've been giving me a crash course in what actual strength looks like. Not being foolishly stubborn for no good reason, letting yourself feel and hope even when that hope is dashed, and finding a way to stand up again. I've never seen anything like it. And I would have told you that I'm the kind of man who would never believe in miracles, but I do."

He moved his hand from beneath hers so he could pick up the one on top, her left. "You are the greatest miracle that has ever happened in my life," he told her, his voice raw. "There's no possible way that I would ever have let myself love that baby the way I think we both know I do, and did from first sight, if you hadn't shown me how it was done."

Her eyes were filled with emotion again, and Knox wouldn't have been surprised if his were too.

"I love you," he said again. "And I don't intend to make you doubt that another moment for as long as we live. There is not one thing in my life that isn't better with you next to me, Ramona, and whether we travel to every single nook and cranny in this world as a family or we stay right here in Cowboy Point and grow roots together, it doesn't matter to me. The only thing that does is you."

But he didn't want her to think he didn't understand that she had every reason to tell him she was done, despite all the things he was saying. He kind of assumed she might.

He said them anyway. "I don't deserve another chance from you. I don't deserve for you to even listen to me say these things. But if you give me one last chance, I swear on my life and on the life I want to show Hailey, and hopefully her mother, too, that I will never not choose you again."

She pulled in a ragged breath, and he slid that ring on her finger. It fit her like it was made for her. It gleamed. It was unique and strange and it suited her perfectly.

"I want to see you every day for the rest of our lives," he told her. "I want my mausoleum of a house to be our house, and I want you to teach me how to make it bright with all of these feelings. I want you to feel claimed by me, needed by me, worshiped by me, every hour of every day you draw breath."

It was almost like he couldn't tell where she began and he ended. That was how intense this was. That was how real this was. He kept going. "You are the love of my life, and I cannot believe it took me so long to accept the truth that I'm pretty sure hit me like a sledgehammer that very first night."

"Well," she said after a minute, and her smile was a little damp but it was the brightest one he'd ever seen, "I *think* that I'll forgive you."

"Will you?" he asked.

He felt like he was caught in a held breath.

Everything depended on what she did next.

Ramona's gaze was brilliant now. She looked down at the ring on her finger, then she lifted that same hand and slid it to hold the side of his face.

"I'm pretty sure I will," she told him, though her eyes were gleaming. "There's just one catch."

"Anything," Knox told her, and it was a hoarse, heartfelt vow.

"It's going to take a long time," she told him solemnly. "There might have to be legal ramifications. In the form of binding ceremonies, if you know what I mean. A long, long time, Knox. I'm thinking… forever, if that works for you?"

And he knew that later, he would think back and understand that this was the day that he'd become the man he'd always wanted to be. The man he always should have been.

All because she trusted him one more time.

"Forever sounds like a perfect amount of time for me to try to make it up to you," he told her, and he dared to smile. "Let's start right now."

Down below, the community of Cowboy Point started counting down to the new year in the half-finished Lodge, but up in this little nook with the lights of their little valley gleaming in on them from afar, Knox and Ramona made a promise.

One that they would spend the rest of their lives living up to, with every scrap of joy that they could find.

But first, as the clock struck midnight, they sealed it with a kiss.

Chapter Twelve

IT WAS ALMOST Valentine's Day before Belinda got to throw the Christmas dinner she wanted.

They had long since exchanged all the gifts, but that wasn't the point of it.

"The point," Belinda was muttering at him as she charged around that morning, putting things to rights, "is all of us spending time as a family. This time, with extra family."

Zeke suspected that might be the real issue igniting his beloved today. Once Ramona's parents heard that their daughter was going to marry a Montana cowboy and truly settle down with him in Cowboy Point, they hadn't wasted any time making plans to come out and visit.

It turned out that Belinda and Bettina Taylor knew each other from childhood. Belinda had actually babysat for Bettina, which had made all the brothers laugh—and then demand that Ramona's mom tell them what Belinda had been like as a bossy older girl who could tell Bettina what to do.

That was effectively the Belinda experience, Bettina had said, earning the Careys' affection forever.

Belinda, on the other hand, had ordered them all outside to shovel the yard and the drive, so that their guests would feel more comfortable.

Her justice was always swift.

It had been a purely delightful New Year so far, Zeke thought, as he settled in at the kitchen table and waited for his family to come pouring in.

The little twin girls, Holly and Ivy, weren't giving their parents much sleep but they were so cute that it was hard to be resentful. Zeke and Belinda had hated seeing the older boys go back home, but they took comfort in the fact that theirs was the kind of family that spent a lot of time with each other. Those boys would grow up running back and forth between their parents' house and their grandparents' house. Soon enough, their sisters would join them.

"Or outrun them," Belinda liked to say with a sniff.

Harlan and Kendall had announced only the other day that they were pregnant again, though it was early days. Little Kiel was only four months old but both Kendall and Harlan looked so pleased with themselves that it was impossible not to cheer them on.

"There's a reason that folks like at least eighteen months between babies," Belinda liked to mutter as she banged around in her kitchen. "I preferred two years."

"Maybe they just want a lot of babies," Zeke usually felt compelled to reply.

Wilder and Cat were focused on her studies, and a whole

lot of aunting and uncle-ing around the ranch. Boone and Sierra were focused on the dairy and the big plans they had for the new summer season.

And Knox, the baby of the family who no one had really believed would ever settle down, had officially become Hailey's only legal parent following the termination of Shoshana Delaney's parental rights.

Zeke was proud of the fact that Ramona and Knox had offered the girl help to build her own life, and she'd been strong enough and determined enough to take it. They'd gotten her out of her questionable living situation and into somewhere safer and better. The last he'd heard, Shoshana was working on finishing high school.

And who knew what she would do then.

Knox had also made it clear that there was an open door for the girl whenever she wanted to see the baby she'd given him. It was up to her.

Zeke admired it.

At the same time, pretty much the day after Shoshana's parental rights had been revoked, Ramona had started the adoption process. Everyone had told them that it would take a long time, so they might as well begin sooner rather than later.

Shoshana had given the doctor a hug and offered her wholehearted blessing.

In the meantime, Knox and Ramona were planning a wedding at the end of June right here in Cowboy Point—

something Bettina had perhaps had a little trouble with, but she was coming around after staying in her father's old house for a couple of weeks and seeing the town as a grown woman, not the eighteen-year-old who had left. The two lovebirds wanted the whole thing on Mountain Mama's patio, on the two-year anniversary of the day they'd met.

Zeke couldn't wait to dance at the last wedding of his last single son.

But that brought up another pressing issue.

That being, his continuing-to-not-die thing.

He noticed how careful everyone was to talk about the future in his presence—meaning they were shutting him out of things for his own protection, and he hated that—and he knew the time had come.

Besides, his work was done.

"I'm still considering telling them that the cancer is in deep remission," he told Belinda as they heard the sounds of voices outside and truck doors slamming shut.

"You do that," his wife replied, making a ruckus on her stovetop. "Or you could be the Zeke Carey I married and own up to what you did."

Then she looked over her shoulder and grinned at him in that wicked way of hers, and he knew that she had absolutely no intention of owning up to anything.

And he was standing there by the stove, kissing his wife deeply and maybe a little punishingly, as the first of the children came trickling in.

"Pull it together, Dad," Harlan said with a laugh. "We have impressionable children here."

"He means me," Boone said, coming in behind him.

Zeke let Belinda go. And then spent the next few hours basking in his dream come true at last.

All of his boys with women they loved, who loved them back just as fiercely. Most of them with children. More on the way.

If there was a better life, Zeke couldn't imagine it.

So after they'd all talked and visited and competed with each other to entertain Ramona's parents with the best stories of Knox as a younger man—all, Zeke noted, stories that celebrated Knox instead of teasing him in any way, almost like they'd learned something now that the good doctor was on the scene—and after they'd all eaten entirely too much of Belinda's pies, he stood up.

He waited for all their eyes to come to him. Zeke could admit that he'd always loved a good show.

"I have an announcement to make," he told them.

He looked at all of their faces. Three generations of Careys under this roof that had held so many of their ancestors. He didn't know how any man deserved to be this lucky.

This is your doing too, he told his Alice, in his mind. *This is the path we started.*

Then he looked at Belinda, and smiled at her, because they would be the ones to keep walking this path until they found its end. Together.

But first, he had a confession to make. "Almost two years ago, I gathered you together and told you that I was dying of cancer," he said, getting right to the point. "There's no particularly easy way to say this, so I'll tell it straight. I lied."

And for a moment, there was silence.

Then all pandemonium broke loose.

There were raised voices, shouts, all manner of carrying on—but Zeke saw after a moment that most of them were laughing.

"My first clue was the lack of chemotherapy," Harlan was saying. "Or any doctors' visits whatsoever." Kendall rocked the baby beside him, and laughed—but then, Zeke knew that she'd known the truth for a while.

"Nobody lives with a diagnosis like that for two years," Wilder was saying, and Cat was nodding like this was a topic they'd discussed a million times. "Even I know that."

"We started a betting pool," Ryder said, nodding at Wilder, though he was looking at Zeke. "I figured you'd confess at Easter, because you like a tidy number. Two full years."

"I called him out on it," Boone said in his booming voice. He shook his head. "The healthiest dying man I've ever seen."

"I'll admit that I had my suspicions," Ramona chimed in. "But nobody asked for my medical opinion, so I kept it to myself."

Sierra and Rosie were grinning at each other, making it clear that they'd known, too.

The only one who wasn't laughing was Knox.

"I had no idea," he said when everything quieted down. "I thought you seemed healthy too. It never occurred to me that my own father would *lie* to me about something like that." He stood up, little Hailey in the crook of his arm. "Dad, that was a terrible thing to do." He glanced at his fiancée, and smiled. "But I forgive you."

"I couldn't think of any other way that I would finally get myself some grandchildren," Zeke told them all, unapologetically. "I'd like to say that I regret what I did, but I don't."

He waved his hand around the kitchen, taking in everybody sitting there. This glorious pageant of life that had started long before him and would last long after he was gone.

His true legacy.

"All of our lives are better for it," he said. "And I'm delighted to say that I will die a happy man."

He lifted up his glass, and toasted them, all of his beautiful children, and their children, and the bright future that he intended to share with all of them and his marvelous wife, for as long as he had left.

Then Zeke Carey grinned. "Just not anytime soon."

The End

If you enjoyed *A Christmas Baby for the Cowboy,*
you'll love the other books in…

The Careys of Cowboy Point Series

Book 1: *The Cowboy's Mail-Order Bride*

Book 2: *The Cowboy's Forbidden Bride*

Book 3: *The Cowboy's Secret Babies*

Book 4: *The Cowboy's Best Friend*

Book 5: *A Christmas Baby for the Cowboy*

Available now at your favorite online retailer!

More Books by Megan Crane

Family Matters of Cowboy Point series

Book 1: *The Cowboy's Least Likely Bride*

The Flint Brothers Take Montana series

Book 1: *Tempt Me, Cowboy*
Book 2: *Please Me, Cowboy*
Book 3: *Tempt Me Please, Cowboy*

The Greys of Montana Series

Book 1: *Come Home for Christmas, Cowboy*
Book 2: *In Bed with the Bachelor*
Book 3: *Project Virgin*
Book 4: *Most Dangerous Cowboy*
Book 5: *Have Yourself a Crazy Little Christmas*

Other titles

A Game of Brides
I Love the 80s
Once More with Feeling

Available now at your favorite online retailer!

About the Author

USA Today bestselling, multi-award-nominated, and critically-acclaimed author Megan Crane has written more than 145 books, and shows no sign of slowing down. She publishes romance as **Megan Crane** and **M.M. Crane** with an exciting backlist of women's fiction, rom-coms, chick lit, and young adult novels. She's also won a large and loyal fanbase as **Caitlin Crews** with Harlequin Presents, Harlequin Dare, Harlequin Historical, and contemporary cowboy books. And for paranormal fun, Megan partners with Nicole Helm to publish as **Hazel Beck** for her witchy rom-com novels.

Megan has a Masters and Ph.D. in English Literature, has taught creative writing classes in places like UCLA

Extension's prestigious Writers' Program, and is always available to give workshops (or her opinion). She lives in the Pacific Northwest with her comic book artist husband, though, at any given time, she is likely to either be huddled in a coffee shop somewhere or off traveling the world. Preferably both.

Thank you for reading

A Christmas Baby for the Cowboy

If you enjoyed this book, you can find more from all our great authors at TulePublishing.com, or from your favorite online retailer.

TULE
PUBLISHING

Printed in Dunstable, United Kingdom

70201281R00127